A Novel

Isaac Perry

Paradox Media Press

CHICAGO

ALL FALLS DOWN
Copyright © 2008 by Isaac Perry
All Rights Reserved
1st Edition

This is a work of fiction. Names, characters, places, and incidents either are the product of the author's imagination or are used fictitiously. Any resemblance to actual persons, living or dead, events, or locales is entirely coincidental.

The ALL FALLS DOWN logo is a registered trademark of Paradox Media.

A portion of this work previously appeared in *Avenue Report* (April 2008).

Published in the United States by Paradox Media Press.
For more information contact:
Paradox Media
PO Box 498552 Chicago IL 60649
Email: info@paradoxmedia.net
www.allfallsdown.com
www.isaacperry.com

Library of Congress Control Number: 2008927503

ISBN-13: 978-0-9816686-0-4
ISBN-10: 0-9816686-0-7

Jacket Design:
Creative Direction by Ray Butts
Art Direction & Design by Kevin Will Chen

Printed in the United States of America by Morris Publishing
3212 East Highway 30
Kearney, NE 68847

Pop—

This book is for you.

Since you've been gone, everyday has represented a different struggle. Sometimes I pause and feel the weight that I know you must have felt. But I don't pause long because I know what's at stake.

I want you to know that I've tried hard to do the things you taught me to do and stand the way you taught me to stand. Your absence has continued to teach me in the same way your presence did.

But I miss you.

Sometimes I forget you're not here anymore and I have to catch myself. I feel as close to you as I ever did, maybe even closer.

It's clear to me that you're the reason I'm a writer. I thank God first, but after Him I thank you for pushing me to develop my love for words and art. I'll never forget what you sacrificed. I'll always try to do the same with Paris.

I looked up on my wall the other day and saw this poem by Assata Shakur called 'Story'.

You died.
I cried.
And kept on getting up.
A little slower.
And a lot more deadly.

I'll never stop getting up, Pop. I promise.

I love you. More than I can say.

Isaac

ONE

Everything in the suite was white. There was a nearly translucent carpet, white sculpture, furniture, and floor-to-ceiling windows that took up the entire far wall. The room was vast and ethereal. I felt removed from myself in a way that I'd read about in stories of the afterlife.

The bodyguard who'd let me in went out the same way. I smelt jasmine around me. A mirror a few dozen feet to the right showed me in the hotel penthouse, alone and dressed in a black suit, the only black thing in a milk-white dream. I cleared my throat and looked around but no one else appeared. Ten minutes went by. Feeling annoyed and uncomfortable, I walked over to a sitting area and plopped down on a couch. I tried to look around the corners of the room that must have lead into more rooms, and then glanced out the windows. I thought about leaving.

The rich—especially the Black rich, who are an anomaly—annoyed the shit out of me. Their cashmere arrogance—all subtle and beautiful, but fused with a heavy ego—inspired my broke-man's pride. I had an allegiance with all the people like me, the broke and struggling, and I was happy not to be tempted by the height of a room like this one. But my desires would always slip in and fuck with my convictions: I had the notion to escape that room but I also had the need to lie down in it, to sleep there and never leave.

I got up and went to the windows along the wall. Past the edge of a stratus cloud I could see the lake, perfectly blue, supple. Down below was the hard earth; cars moving like lethargic insects on the Magnificent Mile. I looked through the clouds again.

"That's my favorite part, too."

The voice shook me. It was smooth, metallic and warm. I turned around and saw a woman I recognized from pictures in magazines and on television. She wore a short dress that was not too different a color than the sky outside and very high-heeled white shoes that, on their own, even without the legs they advertised, would have seemed sexual.

TWO

The night before I'd gone to the penthouse Sydney Barrett called and asked me to meet her at a café on 71st Street. I saw Sydney at a table before going in, her black kinky hair and light skin looking clean and dry through the blur of the rain-soaked window. I went inside and sat down across from her. The waitress came over and I ordered coffee and cake. Gospel music was coming softly from a stereo in the corner. Sydney looked at me with a strange smile and reached across to touch my hand.

"I've got something I want to ask you."

"Somethin' you couldn't ask me over the phone?"

"No," she said. She seemed pleased with herself. "And I've got something to tell you first, before I ask what I need to ask."

The waitress brought my coffee and chocolate cake. I was trying not to look at Sydney's eyes. They'd always been dull, not boring dull, but cool dull; they gave whoever they looked at the feeling that a secret existed between themselves and Sydney.

"Do you remember Daphne?"

"Your friend from LA," I said.

"She's from Chicago, originally. She went to high school with Kayla Forrest. She introduced me to Kayla when I was out there about a year ago."

It had been about a year since Sydney and I had broken up.

"We've become pretty close. We usually talk at least twice a week."

"Really," I said.

"She told me something."

I moved so that I was more comfortable in the chair. I drank some of my coffee and looked out the window.

"Does this have anything to do with her husband?" I asked.

Sydney hesitated. "Yes."

A lead weight dropped softly in my chest. "Go on."

"Kayla asked me for some help. And I thought of you."

The waitress came back to check on us. She was tall, dark brown, with a lonely face. I should have been nicer to Sydney but instead, when the waitress walked away, I let the tips of my gaze brush her all the way back to the kitchen.

Sydney said in a serious voice: "This could be a big opportunity for you, Ellison. This could be *really* big."

"What could?"

"Kayla called me a few days ago. She told me she had something."

ALL FALLS DOWN

Sydney, anxiously excited, leaned across the table and whispered in my ear. Outside, a Metra train was passing and when she finished whispering I could hear the clanging of the warning bells that flashed above the tracks. I leaned back in the chair and looked at her. The bells faded. Sydney's dull-cool eyes met mine over the rim of her raised cup.

"Has she told anyone else about this?"

"She says she told her mother."

"Her mother might have it on the front page quicker than I could."

Sydney smirked. "I need your honest opinion, Ellison."

I narrowed my eyes. "For what?" Then I remembered her saying what her secret could mean for me. "Why'd you tell me this?"

"Kayla called me and asked me what she should do. So, I told her that I didn't know what she should do but I knew someone who *might*. Someone in the media who I trusted."

"And you want me to do what?" I asked. "Advise her?"

Sydney smiled mischievously. "More than that. You could convince Kayla to let *you* be the first one she talks to publicly about this."

I felt the cynic in me rise.

"If she has what you say she has, the last person she's gonna wanna talk to is a reporter."

"That won't be true with you. She knows plenty of media types, but all of them are too close to her, or, more specifically, to her husband. But I told her everything about you. Everyone else she knows is—"

"On the inside," I said.

"Yeah. But being on the outside means you're not under her husband's influence."

"We're all under his influence. Reporters, magazines—everybody who's ever made money off of him is under his influence."

Sydney looked at me warmly but with a tinge of pity. I could see that she still cared about me but we both knew it was done. The distance between us was that distance you feel with everyone you used to love and no longer did. It didn't matter if you were at a table together or in bed, that space would always be there. It was as if your previous intimacy only increased your permanent separation.

"This could work out good for you, El," she said again.

I realized that Sydney didn't pity me; she was nice enough not to do that. But she felt responsible for me. She was trying to hand me a way into her world.

"How's your business going?"

She frowned, knowing that I was taking us off course. "It's excellent. Personal stylists are en vogue. One of my clients is signing a major label deal next week."

I nodded lazily. "Look," I said, "if your friend has what she told you she has, the entire world will want to talk to her. Tell her to call me."

ALL FALLS DOWN

Sydney was happy but she shook her head. "She won't want to talk about it over the phone, though. She's too torn up. The whole thing is terrible."

"That's what makes it sell," I told her.

The stereo had been switched from gospel to jazz. I finished the rest of my coffee and we both got up to leave. Sydney went in her purse.

"I got it," I said. I was digging in my pocket.

"Nope," she told me. "I asked you here."

She let some bills drop on the table. Each one felt like a punch to my stomach.

OUTSIDE IT WAS ONLY RAINING A LITTLE. We walked to Sydney's black BMW truck parked against the curb.

"Do you wanna ride?"

"No," I said, looking around. "I'm gonna walk." The rain was standing like crystal globes on top of the BMW's skin. I held the door while Sydney got in.

"I feel really good about this, Ellison. Aren't you happy?"

I laughed. "Why are you so interested? You don't have to worry about me anymore."

"I just wanna see things change for you, El. I know you've been trying."

"I'm good, Sydney. I'm good where I'm at."

A look of disappointment crossed her face. "I don't believe that," she said, shaking her head. "I just don't believe it." She bent down from where she was sitting and kissed me on the cheek. "Goodnight, Ellison."

"Goodnight, Syd."

I walked the two blocks to my building, went in, and looked through some files I kept on him even though I hadn't interviewed him yet. Inside the manila folder were various news clippings and some notes I'd made to myself. I put one of his CDs on and lay on the couch listening to it. I touched my cheek more than once, thinking about Sydney and what she'd said and the way she'd smelt. I lay there until the sound of the rain on the window and the song John Forrest was singing became similar, and then the same.

THE NEXT MORNING THE DAY WOKE UP and split itself between sunshine and cold. The cold was in the blue of a sky so hard looking the clouds seemed to be nailed to it.

My novel-in-progress had been sitting on my desk like a stepchild. I worked on it for a few hours and then looked at my work dock. I had two articles due that month and that was good. The month before there had only been one thing to work on, which meant that the check I was expecting wasn't going to pay my bills. I was two months behind on rent. I'd already gotten the notice to appear in court.

Anger, as usual, simmered just below my subconscious. It was beneath the surface of every thought: a frustration built from years of living on the edge of poverty, constantly wondering where the next check would come from, how to pay the next bill when the old ones were past due, trying to maintain sanity and stay afloat in a surge of life.

I saw faces like mine in my neighborhood. They floated by, unique yet attached by a chain that stretched back to the last millennium. We shared a similar pain the way we shared stop signs or sidewalks, taking our turn circling the same block of disillusionment. We had all arrived at this point of frustration because we had never departed from it. Poverty remained like a poltergeist. Many of us thought we had rid ourselves of it but still it haunted and disturbed, hurting relatives if not us. Its touch—whether faint or strong—was present in almost every Black life I knew of.

There were the survival skills: benevolent smiles at the work place ("No, really, I'm one of the *good* Black people."), and clandestine emotion, such as never ever letting your white peers know your true feelings about them or your place in their world. You existed in life as invisible as ever, your flesh and blood acknowledged but your identity and culture ignored. I especially felt like a pariah because I was incapable of the corporate politics Black folks needed to succeed in that arena. Because of this I carried in my heart all the bitterness acquired by men who defy the place they are given, and seek to define the place they want.

More and more life looked cynical to me because I couldn't afford a better place to view it from. From my vantage point there were very few joys not affected by the absence of money and success. I had the frustrations of a writer who kept seeing his words erased. I longed for the gratification every artist needs, the confirmation that what he has to say is unique and special, and that someone, *anyone*, feels him. The struggle to be heard dominated my mind and the need to craft my dreams felt like an unavoidable obsession. I was angry at the world yet I had not given up on it because, like every dreamer, I was convinced that the world had plucked me out of the crowd and my struggle was part of my blessing, something to endure until fulfillment would arrive and blot out all my memories of pain.

Sydney called after I ate breakfast and told me where to meet Kayla Forrest. She gave me the address of a four-star hotel on Michigan Avenue. The room number was high enough that I'd probably have to pass a background check to get there.

"When are you gonna get a cell phone?" Sydney asked. "That way you could call me right after you leave Kayla." It was an old joke between us. My list of bills and bad credit had pushed a cell phone pretty far back on my list of priorities.

I went into my bedroom and put on a suit. I never wore suits. I only owned one. But the address required a suit, the woman I was going to meet probably expected a suit, and the opportunity was too great to take any chances. I'd read things about this woman, knew that she was older than her husband. In every picture I could remember seeing her in she looked elegant and professional. I knew a lot about the world I was about

ALL FALLS DOWN

to enter because I'd spent years interviewing its residents.

I finished dressing and left. My apartment was in South Shore, a few blocks from Lake Michigan, what they call an *historic* neighborhood. The wealthy elite had lived here more than half a century ago but now it was our home: lower to middle-class Blacks, mixed with a majority who were by definition poor. It was the kind of place my father had moved us away from when I was a child.

I drove up Lake Shore Drive and twenty minutes later I was passing the towers of the Loop. Before I reached the Mile I passed a building on Ontario where a large picture of John Forrest was painted on the side. It was an age progression, first showing Forrest when he captured the world's attention at 10. Then it followed him through his teenage years, the days when he performed with his brothers and sold more records than any boy band before or after them. And suddenly, against the blue that the artist had chosen to surround the image, John Forrest was a grown man, clutching a microphone as if it had caused him pain and singing into it with eyes closed and sweat sparkling across his forehead.

I parked in a garage and walked slowly down Michigan Avenue. The sunlight was against the sides of the 900 Building. High above my head four boxes that were the color of frost sat in a crown on top of the Four Seasons. I went inside, gave my name to a security guard who looked on a list and smiled when he found me. He picked up a phone and spoke quietly. After that I was escorted to an elevator and went in alone. I rose forever—I imagined passing clouds on my way up—and finally got off and went to the suite number Sydney had given me. I pushed a small button next to a large door and after a few moments a tall, broad-shouldered white man answered—a bodyguard—who opened the door wide and motioned me in.

I went into the white suite and, ten minutes later, watched as Kayla Forrest walked gracefully toward me.

THREE

Her dress was exquisite enough that even I could see it was made from expensive material. If you could turn July into cloth then that's what Kayla Forrest was wearing.

She was a soft bronze and her eyes were among the darkest I had ever seen. There was a heaviness to her face that gave it a little age, and in various ways all her features seemed extreme. Her jaw, her eyes, her mouth, everything was large and lustrous as if drawn abstractly by an artist. On someone who didn't look as good as she did that would have been a bad quality. But on Kayla, whose exaggerated features only heightened the appeal of them, the largeness of her eyes and the excessive nature of her lips and mouth made her sensual. I glanced at her lips and saw that they were in a natural pout. They gave her expression a sense of distaste and I guessed that even when she smiled she would seem unhappy, the sort of sadness that could turn seductive, like pain made into pleasure.

"It's an expensive view," I said, speaking of the outside but keeping my eyes on her.

She ignored the compliment and glanced out the window. I noticed for the first time that she was carrying a drink. Her glass was filled halfway with a blue liquid. When she was in front of me I could see the full maturity of her face; the skin was creamy and smooth but it held character you don't see on women under thirty. Kayla Forrest was thirty-seven, making her eight years older than me and five years older than her husband. I looked at her hair and it was thick and shoulder length and so dark that a literary word about the blackest of black things that I thought I'd forgotten flew into my mind.

The rich woman's hand was suspended in front of me. I took it and we shook. She smiled genuinely.

"It's so nice to meet you," she said. "I'm sorry to have kept you waiting."

Her voice was dark and wet; if it were put into a glass parts of it would stick to the sides.

"Kayla Forrest," she said, still shaking.

"Ellison. Ellison Parker."

"Sydney says you're a journalist?"

"Yes. A writer. I write fiction as well."

She smiled at me again. It should have been a kind, generic smile, but again it was sincere. "That sounds exciting."

I didn't know how to handle her warmth. I felt like a kid blushing under the interest of my relatives. "I do my reporting

ALL FALLS DOWN

mainly for a hip-hop culture magazine called *Swish*. It's based in New York but I'm based here. We cover singers and rappers but we also cover athletes. I just finished a piece on a kid from the city who may be goin' pro next year. I do some freelance for other magazines too, whatever pays the bills." I'm not a big talker so I sounded like I was rambling. "But I'm sure Sydney told you all that."

"She told me," she replied. "But it makes for good conversation."

I looked back out the window. I nodded toward a slope of descending towers. "Views like this are hard to come by."

"No, they're not." She said this too in a warm voice. "Anyone could have this view."

"Could they?"

"Of course." She looked directly at me. "All that's needed is grace, and good manners. Look at those other buildings, Ellison. I can guarantee you that whoever's staring out those windows at us has good manners." She looked outside again and smirked like you do when a funny irony pops into your head. "And if they are wives then they have grace too. They are graceful enough to *keep* this view."

"You're an optimist," I said.

"Are you a cynic?"

"Every time the rent's due."

That made her laugh. She was one of the few women I'd met who was attractive on different levels and you felt those levels

15

before you had time to get to know what they were.

Kayla placed a hand on my arm. She was still smiling when she said: "Let's sit down."

I didn't want to move. We'd been standing close together at the window and it was serene there, with the light from outside right next to her and us seeming like we were standing in the sky.

"Over here."

We went to the white couch. She offered me a drink but I asked for water; it was just past noon.

She disappeared to what must have been a wet-bar hidden behind a partition and came back with a cold bottle of spring water. I was sitting toward the center of the couch and she sat on the end. Huge pillows rested like stars along the space between us. Kayla sipped her drink. She crossed her long legs and leaned back with her elbow against the couch and her head lying against her hand. It was an incredibly casual pose; it could mean that she was at ease with me, or that she was assessing me.

I was about to speak but decided not to. I noticed a painting on the wall behind Kayla and got up to look at it. It was a picture of a Black woman singing, gripping a mike-stand as if it were thunder she was trying to keep in her hands.

"It's a Morris Devaux," Kayla said. "I saw it at his gallery in New Orleans and fell in love with it."

My back was still facing her. "Why?"

She took a moment to answer. "I don't know. It's something

about the mood of it. It just makes me feel strong." She paused. "And angry."

I turned back toward her and sat on the couch. "Tell me what I can do for you."

Kayla's face became a mask. She said dryly, "You know about my husband, of course."

"I know what the public knows," I answered. "He's been accused of having an affair with a young girl, a 16 year-old honors student. She not only gave the cops details about every encounter she and your husband had, she also gave them jewelry he bought for her—jewelry the cops traced back to him—and some pretty explicit letters he wrote. The DA has a good case. A few weeks ago the girl's house burned down. The cops say it was arson. She disappeared. So now you've got on-line rumors that she's dead. I also know the police haven't come out and said they suspect your husband in the arson or the potential murder, but someone will say it eventually." I rattled it all off matter-of-factly and she took it in the same way.

"But what I know that's most important," I continued, "is that if the District Attorney's office doesn't produce this girl soon then the charges against your husband will have to be dropped."

She didn't say anything.

"What I don't know, Mrs. Forrest, is why you asked to see me."

"Call me Kayla, Ellison."

"Kayla."

She gave me a strange look. "It must be interesting for you."

My expression said I didn't know what she meant.

"Your job. Interviewing all those entertainers. Rich and famous people. It must be interesting to always see that."

"You mean, because my life is so different."

She laughed. I felt for a second that she was laughing at me. "I guess it could be irritating too. To be so close, and so far away."

"This is America," I said, trying to sound dismissive. "The success of one man feeds the aspirations of another."

I waited for her to answer my original question. She stopped trying to read me and went back to sipping her drink. After a moment she looked down nervously into it.

"I need your advice."

"I'm listening," I said patiently.

"Something was sent to me. I told Sydney it was OK to tell you about it."

"She did."

"And she said I could trust you."

"And you trust Sydney."

"And I trust Sydney."

"And she told me about the disc."

Kayla breathed deeply. Her eyes closed and I watched the air blow past her thick lips. Suddenly she opened her eyes and spoke in a burst of emotion.

ALL FALLS DOWN

"I don't know why anyone would send me something like that! I don't know where they'd get it!"

She looked as if she might cry. I didn't know how I'd play that if it happened.

"I don't know either," I told her. "Maybe I should see it first, before we go on."

She looked at me with dark, searching eyes. "Do you think that's necessary?"

"You want my advice, right? Let me see what we're talking about."

She was silent. I looked over the back of the couch; saw the sky turn indigo against the windows. Kayla sat back, some form of resolve coming across her face, and picked a piece of lint from the cloth of her skirt.

"It's in the guest bedroom," she said lazily. "In the drawer below the television. I didn't want it in my room."

I followed the direction she indicated and went down a short hall, found two doors, one closed and one not, and went in the open door. It was a guest room nearly as large as my apartment with a plasma television mounted against the wall. Underneath was a bureau. I found a disc inside, slipped into a plain case. I put it in the DVD player and sat down on the edge of a chair. I glanced out the windows and saw the tops of several smaller buildings receding into the gray expanse of city. Then I heard a moaning sound come from the television.

Images of a young girl and John Forrest were there, made

blurry at first and then clearing, and what followed was an obviously amateur recording of Forrest and the girl having sex. She was definitely young; I paused the disc at several points trying to get a closer look at her face. Her body was mature, could have belonged to a twenty-five-year-old, but the adolescent firmness of her breasts and the lack of a grown woman's softness showed that she was younger. I skipped ahead and saw that the disc contained several interludes, in different settings around the same room or rooms, but all of them were with John Forrest and the same girl. I finally got a good look at her face: she could have been fifteen. She glanced into the camera at one point as if she knew it was there but didn't want to show it, and in the glimpse of her eyes I saw an intelligence that flashed like the quick reflection of sunlight off glass.

I tried not to look at John Forrest. It was surreal, seeing someone so much larger than life engaged—however wrongly—in an act as common to all of us as sex. I kept hearing his voice even though he wasn't talking. His moans of gratification sounded to me like the sighs of his songs. I realized that one of the reasons he was such a great singer was that he truly believed in what he sang; it was all there, the joy and tragedy of dozens of his songs, reenacted on the body of this little girl in a performance that was both profound and disturbing.

I turned the player off and went back into the front room. Kayla Forrest had made herself more comfortable. Her shoes sat like obedient children next to the couch. Long legs were

ALL FALLS DOWN

stretched out on the cushions, bare feet resting in the space I'd been sitting in. The look on her face said it all: she was drunk. Not silly drunk or at-the-club drunk. Her expression was careless. My guess was that she was drinking to become numb to what was happening all around her: the infidelity of her husband caught on video, the accusations, the falling down of a world built on the assumed indestructibility of money.

FOUR

At that moment the hotel penthouse was full of opportunities.

A voice spoke inside my head and tried to give me some advice: *Do this shit right, El. Tell her what she need to hear.* But I waited for her to speak first. I didn't want to seem too anxious.

There's the old saying about opportunity knocking but when you're broke opportunity doesn't knock, it calls in a whisper from the sidewalk that is outside the building that is outside your door, asking you to open up the gates of poverty and let it in. It's up to you to recognize opportunity's call. Its voice is so seldom heard you may miss it if you're not careful and it will be drowned out by the cacophony of everyday hood life. But it's there, beneath the sounds of crazy cab drivers, buses squealing, ghetto girls talking loudly on curbs, music bumpin' from slow cars, laughter, el trains: opportunity slips through. I was watching it enter my life through the words and actions of others. It whispered through the loud distractions of my world and I wanted it to know that I was ready to scream back.

ALL FALLS DOWN

I stood next to the couch looking down on Kayla Forrest, a woman who was worth at least two or three hundred million, half of her husband. I saw that her legs were too skinny at the calf but became round and thick at the thigh. She had slender feet and her toes were polished with clear paint. The fingers that held her glass were long. Her face was turned away from me and the line of her profile was smooth but extreme, like the skyline seen from a distance. Finally she looked up at me. The pools of her eyes were deep and rich and held an air of disdain mixed with a plea for understanding.

"I asked you here for a reason," she said in a voice meant to make me feel like her employee.

I relaxed my stance a little then sat down in the big chair next to the couch. "I know," I said. "I'm just trying to get an understanding of exactly what kind of advice you want."

"Someone sent me that disc for a purpose. Either because they want me to know my husband is guilty or because they want him in jail."

"Or both. Or extortion. But your husband could always claim the video was altered."

She gave me a silly look. "You're not naïve, Ellison." She swung her legs slowly off the couch then brought them up underneath her. "We both know that was John." She took a shallow breath. "And that was the 16-year-old I saw in court. They can't print her picture in the newspaper 'cause she's a minor. But that was her. Besides, I recognize those rooms they were in.

It's an apartment John keeps in the city."

"Whoever sent this didn't send anything else? Just the disc?"

Kayla got up and went to another room. When she came back she was holding a folded piece of paper. She sat again on the couch and handed me the paper.

The words had been typed with an old-fashioned typewriter. I could feel the indentations on the other side. It read:

NEXT VIDEO POLICE

I looked the message over again, carefully, as if there was some meaning hidden in its brevity. I asked her: "This came with the disc?"

"Yes."

"And who sent you the disc?"

"I told you I don't know."

"How long ago did this happen?"

She thought for a moment. "I got the disc in the mail last Thursday."

"Here?"

"No," she answered. "They sent it to our house on the North Shore. John wasn't home. It was addressed to me. I left the next day and came here. I keep this suite for whenever I want to come and stay for awhile in the city."

"So he knows you're here."

"Yes. He hasn't called, though."

ALL FALLS DOWN

I thought that was strange but I let it go. I was concentrating on something else. "What else?" I said.

"There's nothing else."

I looked at her with disbelief. "The whole *world's* wonderin' whether or not your husband slept with this girl. You get a DVD of the two of them having sex, and there's nothin' else?"

"I told you what happened," she said.

"You told me you got this disc in the mail. You haven't told me what happened since then."

"Nothing's happened since then." She smirked as if she were amused with herself. "I've just been sitting here."

I asked her: "What kind of choices are you lookin' at?"

"I could take it to the police."

I stood up and went back to the painting of the woman on the wall but I didn't look at her. Instead I stared at the floor and went over a few things in my mind.

Kayla went to the wet bar, fixed another drink and sat down again.

"Don't give it to the cops," I said, "or your lawyers, or anyone else. Not yet."

"What do you think I should do?" she asked. Then she said with only the glimmer of a smile: "Give it to the media?"

I could have tested her then but it wasn't worth it. She was testing me.

"Let me do some digging," I said. "Talk to some people. I think, above all things, you should know who sent it to you."

"I want to know. But I'm starting to wonder if it makes a difference."

"It makes all the difference in the world. Whoever sent it had to be someone close to your husband, or to you. And they have an agenda. Like you said: there's something they want too. You should know what that is."

"I thought about hiring an investigator, but I couldn't trust anyone to keep this from John and his people. No one."

"I know a lot of the people who are around your husband, through the media, PR, and some people in the industry. If there's a rumor about this, if anybody is saying anything at all, I can find out."

"Still," she said, stoically, "I could take it to the police."

I sat down close to her and put on my most comforting voice. "You don't want to do that. If you wanted to do that then you would have already done it. You wouldn't have called Sydney and asked for her help. And you wouldn't have asked to see me when she told you that I could give you some advice. You wanted an objective opinion, right? From someone outside of your husband's influence? If you give that disc to the DA there'll be bootlegs of it all over the streets. It's inevitable. Will that help you? Maybe; if you're going for the divorce settlement. But the fact remains that somebody sent you that disc for a reason. And that's the first thing: find out who sent it and why."

She had been staring at me the whole time with a lost look on her face. I couldn't tell if she was really entranced by what I was saying or off in her own world, thinking about the consequences of her actions, the life she was leaving behind or the one she was returning to. At that moment I thought I might be forced to leave with nothing: no disc, no interview.

Kayla picked up her glass but didn't drink. She thought for a moment and then very plainly said: "He can't go to jail. John Forrest would rather be dead then let anyone put a chain on him. Or tell him he couldn't be who he has always been."

"It could all be moot," I said, "if the girl doesn't show up. Without her there's nothing. Unless the DA gets that disc."

I was trying to keep her somewhere between a desire to find out where the disc had come from and a fear of sending her husband to jail. She had spoken of his fears but I knew that she was speaking for herself too. She would never be poor again but if John Forrest went to jail, much of her life—the glamour and prestige of being his wife—would go with him.

"It could have been Milk," Kayla said abruptly.

"What?"

"It could have been Milk Adderley who sent me the disc."

I waited for her to explain.

"He hates John."

Milk Adderley was a community organizer on the South Side, a kid's summer-league basketball coach, and a cocaine dealer. His associates were heads of Chicago's Black and Latino gangs. These were older men who ruled city blocks from behind the desks of their legitimate businesses. Some of the local press knew who Milk was and they knew he was very close to John Forrest. But that alliance went unspoken, the media was too much in love with their star. Another singer had once told me that Forrest liked the allure of the streets and kept gangsters in his entourage because of the edge they brought.

"Milk is your husband's friend. It's an open secret."

"I didn't say they weren't friends," Kayla answered. "Milk is one of John's few confidants."

"Then what makes you think he would trick on him?"

Kayla shook her head as if to make sense of the theory. "I don't know. But he's jealous of John. I think maybe he always has been." She smiled at me and her eyes were close to laughter. "I asked you if it was hard to be around people like John. I mean, Milk is rich in his own right, but he doesn't have what John does. No one on earth does. I watched my husband become what he is, Ellison. And Milky watched it too. I think maybe we all hate John a little."

"I know Milk Adderley," I said. "I interviewed him once for a story on high school ball."

Kayla got up and went to a table. She sorted through some papers and came back to the couch with a large envelope. She pulled several invitations from it and handed one to me.

"They're giving a party for John's new cologne tonight at Blu 47. His business manager and agent both called me this morning and asked that I be there." She smiled sardonically. "They said it's important for me to be seen as supportive of John."

ALL FALLS DOWN

"Does anyone know that you're living here?"

"I've been discreet."

"So you're protecting him," I said. "Protecting his image."

Her face grew reserved and dignified. She took in a deep breath. "I'm protecting me."

Kayla took the invitation back and found something to write with.

"This is my cell phone number," she told me, scribbling on the back. "A lot of John's people will be at this party. If you wanted to meet any of them."

"That's a good idea," I said.

"If you hear anything, anything about this video, please call me."

"I will. What are you gonna do in the meantime?"

She gave me a warm expression. "You mean: am I going to take your advice and sit on the disc?"

"Yeah."

"I don't know yet. I honestly...don't know."

I'd interviewed enough people to know that was as much as I was going to get. I stood up and noticed that the sun had climbed to its peak and would be sliding westward for the remainder of the day.

"I should go," I said.

She stood up too. She was only an inch shorter than me. Close to her I could smell the jasmine of her perfume and the alcohol on her breath. She gave me a kind smile and I watched the pouting nature of her lips curl into something close to gratitude.

"I really appreciate you coming. And," she hesitated for a moment, glancing down at the floor. Then her eyes looked back into mine. They were cobalt, intense. "Sydney told you: you are not to talk to anyone about this."

It sounded too much like a command. When I didn't answer her she said, in the same measured voice: "I'm trusting you, Ellison, to keep your word."

I smiled at her, a big, affectionate smile. "You got nothin' to worry about."

I tucked the invitation in an inside pocket. I walked to the door and Kayla followed me. I turned around to look her in the face. I said the next few words in a voice that matched the warmth she had shown me all afternoon.

"You can trust me."

FIVE

I got in my car and drove south. My friend, Pablo Dorsey, was in the hospital. I had seen him the week before and wanted to go again. I told myself it was because he was the sick one and because he could use the support, but at that moment I felt the need for some support too.

There was a choice before me but I was hardly aware of it at the time. It was a subtle choice, a place where every slight decision paints a larger picture. I wanted my train of thought—my choice—to be affirmed. I knew on a subconscious level that seeing Pablo would do this for me, if only by showing me the danger of going the other way.

I skipped the expressway and drove through downtown. On the Clark Street Bridge I could see the water of the river trembling as if a giant were walking nearby. I drove the streets just south of the river and passed all the people with ordinary, real jobs, going in and out of offices, establishing futures for themselves and their children. And for only the fourth time that day, maybe just the 603rd or 604th time that year, I wondered if I was doing the right thing. The novel might not sell, just like the last one. The few regular gigs I had as a journalist could fall apart tomorrow. And maybe tomorrow, when I went to court for the late rent I owed, I would be evicted.

But I truly felt that I was doing what I was supposed to be doing; if it was not the right thing, then I wasn't accountable for that. Society didn't know what was right; it only knew its own rules. And I had to have enough faith to follow a different plan. That's what I told myself on good days. On bad days I went through the classifieds.

I pulled onto a side street near Stroger Hospital and found a parking spot. I walked a block or so and saw Cook County Hospital still standing defiantly, proud as an old lion, in front of the newly built Stroger. The old Cook was empty, a great work of architecture hollowed out by time.

I looked up and saw dusk hanging from the shoulders of the Sears Tower. Downtown lights smeared against the evening. I went through the revolving doors at the front of Stroger and found an elevator to take me to Pablo Dorsey's floor.

A nurse was standing outside his room, writing on a clipboard. She was a Latina with long black hair that sat on the shoulders of a blue uniform and her face was very frail but pretty. Latino women had always intrigued me because I had never slept with one. I'd felt that way about Asian women until I spent a weekend with a Japanese girl in San Francisco who told me that she had built the same intrigue around Black men.

ALL FALLS DOWN

The nurse stopped writing and smiled. "Are you here to see Mr. Dorsey?" she asked in a soft tone.

"Is he awake?"

"Just barely. He was talking when I was just in there, but it was sleep talk." Then she said with another smile and a quick, affectionate laugh: "He tried to grab my ass though. I like him."

It would have been an inappropriate thing to say if we were from different worlds. But I'd learned that when hood folk—no matter what hood they're from—are alone together in professional places they sense the hood in each other and let their guards down. She'd sensed South Shore in me and I had sensed what was probably Humboldt Park in her. We'd never met, but the formal atmosphere of the hospital brought us together.

"Everyone likes him," I told her. "I'm his nephew."

We shook hands.

"You don't look nothin' like him," she said.

"You know how it is; it's more a term of affection than an actual blood thing."

"Oh, right."

"I'll be in here for a while," I said. "Where will you be?"

She grinned. "I have a few more rounds to make. But I'll check on Mr. Dorsey later."

"I'll wait for you."

She seemed embarrassed.

I nodded toward the door. "Is he any better?"

The nurse hesitated, not out of any desire to lighten the

blow of a bad report, but simply to check her chart. When she spoke it was in a soft whisper. "I'm not supposed to speak about a patient. Especially if you're not family." She paused. I waited. It was clear that she was going to tell me something. "But since he's been here you're the only person I ever seen visit him." She paused again and then glanced at her chart to double check what she'd seen a moment ago. "They think he'll need another surgery soon. Maybe tomorrow." She put the chart by her side quickly and gave me a blank stare.

"That ain't good."

"I know." She actually seemed sad.

"I'll find you before I leave," I said. The nurse smiled and showed her teeth. Her smile was better without them.

I went into Pablo Dorsey's room. It was small and held two beds. He was the first patient, the one closest to the door, and a green curtain separated him from his roommate. Pablo was asleep. I stood by the bed and watched him. Irregular gasps made his chest rise, pause, and then suddenly collapse with a violent exhalation. There was another pause before it would rise again.

His face was relaxed. His eyes flickered open and looked at me without focusing and then the lids fell back across them. He had dark-brown eyes that were so intelligent they always seemed sad, as if they knew the answer to the riddle that had fooled the rest of us. A heavy moustache, interspersed by white, hung over his mouth. The hair on his head was curly and still

ALL FALLS DOWN

thick. He looked slender and small inside the bed, but his face remained dignified. In certain places, especially around his sad/smart eyes, he looked to be at least seventy years old. If you looked at him as a whole you would think he was beating the cancer.

I turned to walk away. Pablo's voice came from the bed. "Where you goin', young blood?"

"I thought you was sleep."

"I'm up."

I tried to smile. "I just came to see how you was doin'."

"I'm dyin', young blood. Pull up a chair."

I took a *Sun-Times* off a chair and sat down. On the cover of the newspaper was a picture of John Forrest. It was the photo they had been re-running all week, the one from the press conference where he had pointed into the camera and told it he had never had sexual relations with that girl.

"Only shit to interrupt the war," Pablo said about the *Sun-Times* cover. His voice sounded weaker than before, as if he were calling out from another room. "What's more important? The war or the shit that man done got himself into?"

I didn't answer him.

"What you doin' here anyway? You was here last Monday."

"That was Tuesday, I think."

"Whenever. You got better places to be, don't you?"

"Not right now."

"I don't know why anybody wanna keep comin' back here," Pablo said.

The air in the room was tinged with that bland smell hospitals are prone to. The dull colors of the walls and furniture didn't help. A light over Pablo Dorsey's bed shed a halo on him. It was sharp, like the light in a cop's interrogation room, and it made me wonder what questions death could ask you. There was only one other light, an unnatural one that hovered on the other side of the green curtain. I stared at the curtain and the glow, wondering about the man who was on the other side.

"Pablo," I said, "do you remember a cat named Milk Adderley?"

"'Course I do. I been out the game for a minute, but some muthafuckas you never forget."

"Milk was hustlin' when you was out there?"

"Hell no," Pablo answered. "His time came after mine. But I saw him comin' up. He was startin' to make some moves."

Pablo was a playground legend. That's what I always mention about him first. The other stuff doesn't matter as much. What had made him famous was what he did on basketball courts all over the South Side and even the West Side. He became a legend in the 70s and 80s, a prep star that didn't make it in college but played a little pro. I had written a story about him and spent a lot of time with him the year before he got the cancer. The people I spoke to and the old magazines and newspapers I read all described him as the ghetto genius that evolved

ALL FALLS DOWN

basketball into a different form. The story I wrote paralleled him to other geniuses: Charlie Parker, Marvin Gaye, Picasso, and Langston Hughes. But Pablo's story also included his other life, his career as a hustler, a drug dealer, and a pimp. The nickname the courts had given him, the Artist, carried over into the streets and he became a legend there as well. And all that legend was encased in this hospital room, a life that seemed boundless to me held securely in the cheap linen of a deathbed.

"When I was still out there," Pablo added, "they hadn't even started callin' him 'Milk' yet. Can't remember the man's real name. You know why they call him 'Milk'?"

"No."

"His coke, man. Shit seemed to come out his stomach he had so much." He laughed. When he was done he thought for a moment and said, "I remember Price used to hang wit' Milky." Price Ingraham was a friend of ours.

"When was the last time you spoke to Price?"

"It's been a lil' while. He don't play no more and we sort of lost touch."

Pablo coughed and his body racked violently. I moved around in my chair, not sure if I should call the nurse. Then the coughs subsided and Pablo seemed at ease.

"Shit comes on like a light switch."

"What'd the doctors say?"

"They say they wanna do another surgery. Go back in and see if they can get the rest of this shit."

"That's good, right? If they think there's a chance."

"Fuck that." Pablo's voice was hard. "They ain't opening me up no more."

"Maybe you should let 'em try. What you got to lose?"

"Time," he said. "Only got a little time left. Ain't gonna spend it in here."

"Where you gonna spend it?"

He coughed again, this time not so jarringly, and breathed heavily. Neither of us spoke for a few minutes.

"Why you wanna know about Milk?"

"I'm workin' on a story."

He turned his head and gave me a questioning look. I wondered if anyone had ever lied to the Artist and gotten away with it.

"Alright, Ellison. But don't work too hard. Milky is a hard nigga. He got bodies on him."

"I've heard that."

"Believe that. Plus that nigga pushes major weight."

I nodded my head in consideration and then for some reason my thoughts drifted away from the hospital room and went back down the hallways of the Four Seasons, to Kayla Forrest's front door. I began thinking about her slender feet and the thickness of her thighs. Then I was watching the way her lips moved when she talked. They were saying my name repeatedly, smoothing over the 'L' sound and speaking to me in some future time, a time when I lived with her in her Michigan Avenue palace and below us the rest of the world toiled away in futility, just as I had once done. When I finally came back to the hospital I shook my head and made a sighing noise to let Pablo know I was about to leave. "Well, I'd better get going." I got up and threw the newspaper back on the chair.

Pablo looked me up and down. "What you dressed up for?"

"I was workin' on that story."

The older man laughed. It was barely a murmur. "Shiiit, nigga. That must be a hellafied story."

"It might be the best one yet," I told him.

"Can't be better than what you did on me." He said this to compliment himself and to compliment me. The piece I had written on him had established our friendship, mostly because I had managed to understand him through words in a way other writers hadn't.

The tragedy of Pablo Dorsey is that he never played the off-court game, he never learned to sacrifice any part of what he deemed the truth in order to gain any part of what other people said was wealth. Pablo was a ghetto child who scored a 29 on his high school ACT and knew his combination of intellectual brilliance and athletic genius made him different. He was aware that he had a purpose, a special destiny. But in order to achieve it, they—the college coaches, the owners of professional teams, the sponsors and media—told him he would have to conform. His ghetto swagger and militancy would have to be left behind if he was to move forward. His style of play—a style that fused the inner city to basketball in the same way Rap fused the streets to music—didn't mesh with what conventional coaches approved of. So Pablo had a choice: he could play their way, and act the way they wanted him to act when cameras were turned on and mics were in his face; or he could remain true to the fire in his soul and never apologize for what it burned down because, as he told me more than once, the fire inside him "was clearin' a path."

I looked the Artist in his eyes as I got ready to leave the hospital room. "I'll come back soon," I said.

Pablo looked sad.

"Has Mary been here?"

"The first day." His voice was distant again. "The day before you came. Then she said she was goin' home and packing up her shit. Mary don't like hospitals and she don't wanna be around the niggas that's dyin' in them."

I cleared my throat and tried to sound positive. "I'll come back and check on you."

"I'ma be leaving soon."

"You're gonna check yourself out?"

"If that's what I got to do."

"Well," I said, leaving. "I'll be back before then. I'll give you a ride home."

I went to the door and opened it. I turned back to say goodbye again but Pablo had closed his eyes. I saw the other man

ALL FALLS DOWN

move behind the green curtain and the light threw a brief shadow against the cloth. Then I walked into the hallway and closed the door behind me.

I went down the elevator and left the hospital. I forgot to look for the pretty nurse.

SIX

The party Kayla Forrest had invited me to was that night in Bronzeville. I went home to eat and change clothes and while I was there I got two phone calls. The first was from a white man. "Is Eva Vaughan there?"

"Who?"

"Eva Vaughan, please."

"You got the wrong number, man."

"Are you sure?"

"You got the wrong number."

"Could you look for her?"

"What?"

"Could you look—"

I hung up.

I took off my jacket and tie and put my dinner in the microwave. When I was almost done eating the phone rang again. It was Sydney.

"What happened with you and Kayla? You were supposed to call me back."

ALL FALLS DOWN

"Everything was cool. I'm sure she told you about it."

"She called me crying."

"What for?"

"She says she's going to the police."

"Why?"

"Is that what she told you?"

"No. I told her to hold off on that."

"Call her, Ellison. She may listen to you."

I took a sip of grape juice. "Why are you so interested in this, Syd? What difference does it make to you what this woman does?"

"Just call her, Ellison." Her tone was stern. She spoke like a parent who was tired from the effort it took to prod their child onto the right path.

"You didn't answer my question," I said, my own voice suddenly hard.

"You're not taking this seriously enough. You don't understand—" she paused. "You don't understand what this could do."

"Is there something you're not telling me, Syd? Are you somehow involved in this?"

I heard her smile through the phone. It was an ironic smile, something she did whenever I hit on a truth that was more potent than I knew.

"I'm involved. Through you."

"What's that mean?"

"It means that if you're successful, so am I."

"You're there, Syd. You already made it. You don't have to wait for me no more."

Sydney's voice sounded frustrated. "Don't you understand?" She paused again, this time to keep herself from getting too angry. I waited.

"I love you, Ellison."

"Good, but—"

"And I want you to know what it feels like, to know how it should be and how it should—, how you should...be."

"I told you before that I'm where I wanna be."

"And I told you I don't believe that," Sydney said.

I thought about my next words carefully. "I'm gonna succeed, Syd; whether I talk to Kayla Forrest today or if she never speaks to me again. Do you believe that?"

Sydney waited too long before saying, "Yes."

There was a long moment of silence, a silence filled with four years of love and disillusioned loss. Finally Sydney decided to pull us both out of the quiet fire. "Are you going to the party they're having tonight?" she asked.

"Maybe," I said.

"I guess I'll see you there." We hung up without saying goodbye.

I took out the invitation Kayla had given me and copied the cell number she'd written on the back onto a separate piece of paper. Then I examined the invite, looking closely at its design. It

ALL FALLS DOWN

was worth a lot to the hundreds of journalists and socialites who probably hadn't made the guest list. An industry party in honor of John Forrest was an event rare and exclusive enough to spark the desires of every celebrity and celebrity reporter in town.

I thought about the white man who had called earlier and then I dialed Kayla's cell number to ask if she'd spoken to anyone about me, or the fact that I was helping her. The call went to voicemail but I hung up without leaving a message. The white man's voice saying *Eva Vaughan* was playing in my head like a song I'd heard on the radio.

I went into the bedroom and lay across the bed. I reached underneath and pulled out a box full of old letters. I found a picture of Syd on the 63rd Street beach. After we'd sat on the beach we'd gone to watch the old men who were playing African drums beneath the trees. After the sun went down it felt like it was going to rain; I remembered the wind blowing stiffly through the leaves. Sydney and me listened to the drums and her hips began to sway and *Muntu* with the beat. Birds circled above lazily and a warm feeling spread through my body when I realized they were gliding on the groove.

By the time the sky was black and mad we were back home making love. I didn't wait to get her in the bedroom. We did it on the floor of the dining room where I had no dining table. The way she held on to me, gripped me, was so free with me, it was one of the few times in my life when I knew exactly how much a woman loved me.

o o o

I TOOK OFF THE REST OF MY SUIT and put on a pair of black pants, a button-up and a thin black coat. I looked in the mirror and approved myself for the night, though I wondered about the other people who would be there, the rich folks and their rich clothes.

I drove up Lake Shore Drive to 47th Street. Before I could get to the restaurant I came up on a police barricade. A cop pointed north and I turned that way and parked near an alley. I walked back through the alley, went another block westward past the barricade and came into a crowd.

There must have been four thousand of them.

They stretched from 47th on south and the cops had blocked off enough streets to keep them contained in one area. Which meant that the city had not only known about this, they helped plan it. The crowd of thousands was surrounding one object: a video screen the size of a small skyscraper erected in the intersection of 47th and King Drive.

The screen reached a height of at least fifty feet and thirty feet across. I couldn't see where the images that flashed across it were being projected from, but the effect of it was chilling. The faces of everyone standing on the sidewalk and in the street were a flicker of monochromatic color: a pale-blue wash that was the digitized shadow of John Forrest.

Television news trucks were parked against the curb and crews and reporters were broadcasting live from the street. They

ALL FALLS DOWN

filmed the enormous crowd, a motley crew of neighborhood people mixed with the industry types who had come to Blu 47 for the party.

I looked up at the screen. The giant silhouette of John Forrest's slender body, a darkened shape without features framed against a background of swirling colors, held a microphone and performed in a flow of movement that deserved as much documentation as the *Kama Sutra*. The silhouette was for dramatic effect; it made the ad more powerful and played into the singer's mystique. His music wafted from giant speakers, his voice soared and sent notes disappearing into the night like blackbirds. The bump of the bass-line made the street tremble. And every sharp move he made on the screen translated into a joint sigh or round of applause from the crowd, all of whom stared at the screen in unison with awe stretching their features into expressions that would have looked silly anyplace else.

After the commercial ended, the logo for Forrest's new cologne illuminated the screen like a national flag. Then another commercial played. Three in total, in a loop, all similar to the first one. The crowd screamed its joy. I thought about what Pablo had asked, if the war wasn't more important than the life of John Forrest. It was strange knowing that those kind of things could be equally important to so many people; whether 9/11 would happen again, whether our armies should be in Iraq, whether we'll get our first Black president, whether John Forrest should be in jail. Then I heard an old neighborhood woman standing next to me whisper, "God bless him" as she looked at the video screen and I walked away.

I passed the crowd control cops who stood at the fringes of the celebration and went toward the restaurant. A valet was taking control of the cars and cabs that slid to the curb. There was a small mob in front of the restaurant as well, people trying to get in and bouncers and ushers checking invitations and turning people without them away. A phalanx of paparazzi took shots for the tabloids and magazines.

A bouncer told me: "Private party! You got an invitation?"

I showed it to him.

The man studied it. "Let me see your ID."

I gave that to him too.

"A'ight."

I walked with two women dressed in beige to the elevator. We all got on and went to the second-floor entrance of Blu. We stepped into a hallway whose left wall was painted a dark color that was softened here and there with strokes of dull white. It reminded me of snow when it's early in the morning and the only thing that's touched it is moonlight. Along the wall were paintings of jazz characters blowing trumpets and playing pianos in abstract shapes. I stopped to get a better look at them.

A maitre d' went by, on his way back into the restaurant and said: "You know about the gallery right? In the next room?"

"Na," I said. "I've never been here before."

"It's right through those doors. You can order something

ALL FALLS DOWN

from the bar and bring it in with you." He went back down the hall.

I looked at the paintings for a while longer and then followed the maitre d's path into the restaurant. Four men were coming out, two of them talking on phones. I waited for them to pass and I stepped inside Blu 47.

SEVEN

I saw **Milk Adderley** almost immediately. The gangsta, the summer-league sponsor, had his arm around the shoulders of another man and was talking to him, his mouth right next to that man's ear. His free hand was making very strong, definite gestures in the air. Whatever point he was making was being taken in syllable by syllable: the man whom he was talking to kept nodding his head every other second as if he were one of those bobble toys they hand out at arenas. Milk was a big cat and the other man was tall and skinny. The skinny man wore a black, pinstriped suit. He had a hawkish black face where, above a thin nose, two narrow eyes were staring at the floor so as not to be distracted by anything visual while Milk was giving aural information to the ear. I watched as Milk finished speaking, gave the man a hard pat on the shoulder with the hand that had been hanging there, and turned to walk away. The thin man went off in a different direction.

I thought about following Milk but I needed to work out an angle first. There was no use in talking to him unless I could figure out a way to open up the conversation. I thought about casually mentioning the rumor of a disc, but I'd have to be careful. I had no idea what Milk's involvement was.

I ordered a rum & Coke and stood at the bar. I noticed logos from the Forrest cologne everywhere, on napkins and even coasters. Undaunted by the bad press surrounding the threat of a trial, John Forrest's endorsement deals had kept things moving. They were ignoring the controversy and going ahead with their plans to maintain his place in culture. From what I'd heard from people in the industry, it was working.

The restaurant was full of the smell of *Fire*, Forrest's cologne—the test bottles having been opened and used by nearly everyone. It was a unisex scent that the company said would take on the personality of each individual wearer and fuse it with the essence of Forrest, therefore turning any ordinary man or woman into "a star." I thought about trying some but I was already wearing a different scent.

I took my time with the drink and looked around. A few people I knew came over to talk. Everyone seemed to be enjoying themselves. I realized that this was not just John Forrest's party. It was a celebration held for everyone who had leapt over the obstacles and survived the frustrations that had tried to force them out of this restaurant and into the streets, into neighborhoods like the one a few blocks from here where people weren't drinking martinis or kissing each other on the cheek. Yet it seemed everyone there had a hidden fear. It was a fear a Black person experienced whenever they gained any form of success. It was the fear that this could all be over, that the lights could come on at any moment and everything gained in the dark would vanish. I looked around me at the city's Black elite, and despite their money and free attitudes, they were still trapped by a faraway past. It was as if their lives were on loan and every person at Blu 47 that night was a Cinderella. At some hour the Benzes and Hummers parked in the valet lot would turn to watermelons and America would beckon home its stepchildren.

Damn.

I wasn't just broke and unknown: *I was a hater too.*

I smirked and took a sip of the rum. Jazz flowed from the band in the corner of the room and the trumpeter played a solo. When it burned out, the piano came from the ashes, took over the song, and ended it with a rush of keys that sounded like birds leaving a windowsill.

I saw Price Ingraham standing by the alcove that led to the VIP section. It was Price who Pablo had told me hung with Milk Adderley. And I knew Price better than I knew Milk. So I went over.

Price saw me coming and his face lit up. We clasped hands and pulled each other into a hug. We had once spent a long day together rolling around the different blocks surrounding the Pocket, the neighborhood where he first learned to play ball. I was profiling him for a story. We talked about everything from basketball to the US involvement in the drug trade. Price was

ALL FALLS DOWN

that kind of cat. I wrote a story on him entitled "The Final King" for *Swish*. It was about the dying art of playground basketball.

"Where you been?" he asked me.

"I been around."

"*Bull*shit. I ain't seen you in forever! You still write for *Swish*?"

"They keep tellin' me I do."

"I feel you," Price said. He was looking me up and down.

"You know Pablo's in the hospital," I said.

"I heard that. Heard it around."

"He told me he ain't seen you in a minute."

Price shook his head. "It's fucked up what happened to the Artist, man. People don't understand. No one eva' played ball like that. No one gonna play like that again."

"You should holla at him."

Price furled his eyebrows. He was a good lookin' cat. He wasn't very tall, though. Around my height: an inch under six feet. He had dreadlocks that fell almost to his shoulders.

"I'ma try," he told me.

"What happened between the two of you anyway?"

"I don't know," he answered. "I think maybe hangin' too hard with Pablo got me worried. You know he was strung out for a while. I couldn't believe it when he started usin' that shit. After that he tried to chill. Tried to do everything by the books. But I don't know if a cat like that can switch up, E."

"He was doin' all right."

"You think so?"

"But cancer don't give a shit who you are."

"Come on," Price said. He took me by the arm. "We gotta table over here. This is a party. Don't nobody want to stand around talkin' 'bout death."

I noticed the faint scar that ran down the side of Price's face. A girlfriend who had cut him with a razor during an argument put it there. I remembered that the girlfriend had disappeared the day before Price got out the hospital; his alibi was solid.

We went into the VIP to a table gorgeous with burning candles and women. On the walls was more of the artwork I had noticed in the hallway: Jazzmen washed in tones of blue and indigo and so abstract that in the flicker of the candles they somehow made sense. Milk Adderley was sitting underneath one of the portraits. His size dominated the table. There were other men and women there too that I didn't immediately notice. Finally my eyes went to a woman wearing a red dress sitting next to Milk.

Price sat down in a chair and introduced me.

"I remember you," Milk said. His voice was a baritone accented with an elegant tenor. "The writer."

"I interviewed you for that piece on Chicago preps. The Red South."

"Right." He had a cigar in his mouth that he took out from time to time. "I remember that shit."

I tried to keep my eyes off his woman but it was useless. It

ALL FALLS DOWN

wasn't that she was any more beautiful than some of the other women in the restaurant; there was another quality to her, something very different, and rare. She had honey colored skin and her hair was done up in auburn curls that rippled to her shoulders and breasts. Her face was small and fine featured. Her nose turned slightly upward and her small mouth was open so that the lips—which were the color of a coral reef—let me glimpse a ridge of white sand teeth. When her eyes rose up to me they held the quality that seemed to grip her whole body in a soft vice: innocence. That's what made her rare and so interesting to me. The demure expression on her face and the subtle quality of her beauty made her look out of context with everyone else she sat with. I'd seen women like her before, models in the stacks of *Travel + Leisure* I had in my apartment. They lay next to unheard-of beaches in Anguilla; rode the backs of brown elephants in Africa; walked the streets of Moorish cities in Spain. I felt distrustful of her type of beauty, the type that seemed so truthful that it had to be a lie. Maybe before then, when I believed in a whole lot of things, I could have believed in a woman like that. But at the time she could only be tolerated in magazine spreads. You stared at her, enjoyed her, and turned the page.

 I tried to engage Milk Adderley in conversation. The big man wore D&G glasses that had a rose-tinted shade. His high-yellow skin was pockmarked here and there and held lines of age. His hair was short but curly. He wore a cream suit with an Irish-green tie and handkerchief and had shiny rings on his thick fingers. He waved his cigar while he talked, leaving lines of smoke hanging in the air like quotation marks.

"I got some good kids," he was saying. "Most of 'em live in homes without they daddy. So all the time their mothers are comin' up to me and askin' me to do somethin' with them. So I do: we teach them ball, and we try to teach 'em life."

I nodded my head, pretending to be engrossed. I didn't want to bring up anything important. The setting wasn't intimate enough for me to believe Milk would talk seriously about anything I needed him to talk about. I'd have to come up with a reason for us to speak later.

Several other people at the table joined our conversation. We were talking pro ball, and specifically the media coverage surrounding it, and the media talk somehow brought us to the Forrest case. Word spread around the table that I was a journalist. Questions came at me about the media's honesty and bias against John Forrest, accompanied with a look. It was a look I'd seen before, on the faces of a lot of Black folks who had complaints about journalism as a whole, especially about the shortcomings of the Black media. They would come to me, shake their heads at my profession and talk to me as if I'd just written a receipt for the Devil.

"Ellison is the truth," Price said, answering a doubtful question that had come at me from somewhere on the other end of the table.

ALL FALLS DOWN

"You sure about that?" Milk asked me. I noticed that he was looking at me strangely.

Before I could answer a loud roar came from the front room. All of us stopped talking and looked toward the VIP entrance. The roar was followed by clapping: a loud rolling applause as if the walls to the restaurant had been torn down and the thousands of fans in the street had climbed inside. Milk Adderley stood up. He went past the girl next to him and left the table without saying a word. The applause became deafening and I could feel it under my chair, like people were beating their open palms against the walls and stomping the floor. Price left the table too. I knew what was going on but I didn't want to move.

I waited for as long as I could and then got up.

It was obvious that John Forrest had finally come to his own party. And like everyone else, I couldn't resist the urge to see him.

EIGHT

It was like I was a kid again. Back when my father would take my brother and me to street fairs in Dayton before we left the hood for the suburbs. At the fairs the people were all taller than me and I couldn't see the passing floats or Black marching bands entirely. But I caught glimpses of them over shoulders and saw the image of giant balloons going past: enormous, colossal, blown full of dream and joy. They were also profoundly mute. They signified more than they could ever say.

My father would put me on his shoulders. I was one of the few kids I knew whose father lived at home. When I was on his shoulders I was eye-level with the balloons. I was as emphatic and high as they were. Standing in Blu 47 I was shoulder-less as hell. And I felt sad thinking about my pops. All those years I'd put so much weight on him. I was almost thirty and I knew about life, the life of a Black man. But as a kid, in my quest to become a giant balloon, I didn't appreciate the height of the man I sat upon.

ALL FALLS DOWN

The crowd at Blu was standing. Everyone's attention was directed toward the area in front of the stage, but I couldn't see. I tried to move around but it was no use. The restaurant was thick.

The applause faded reluctantly and I heard a slight murmur that sounded like someone speaking without a microphone. Whoever was talking spoke slowly and purposefully. Even though I couldn't make out the words I could feel the bass of a voice surround them, giving them power, making me feel as if they were being spoken directly to me.

The murmur increased, the speaker was closing a point, and then the crowd applauded once again. By the time the clapping was over someone had found a microphone but the voice that came across it was not the voice of the first speaker.

The new voice said: "I don't know about y'all, but I just want to give *another* round of applause for this man standing here next to me!"

The crowd complied.

When the noise had died again the voice said: "Thank you, John. Thank you for coming out here tonight in the midst of a busy schedule and helping us celebrate this launch!"

I heard the murmur again. Why didn't someone hand him a mic? The applause came, once more, as drowning as ever. The second voice said: "Thank you. Thank you. John? Do you want...? OK. Well...yes...Let's make sure we—" The man, whoever he was, switched off the mic. It took almost ten minutes for the restaurant to sit down again.

When everyone had settled I remained standing at the rear of the dining room, looking for John Forrest. I guessed that they had escorted him to some secluded table where he could sign autographs and greet people. Then I saw his wife.

Kayla Forrest was standing by a table near the stage, saying something to the people sitting there. She was wearing an orange mohair coat that was light enough to be left on indoors, and on her face were beige aviator sunglasses. Her jet-black hair was straightened. The smile on her face was genuine. She looked beautiful and glamorous. She was just as convincing a saleswoman as the blind lady of justice. Her every gesture was characterized by a very rich, very important aura, as if she were extending herself to people of a lower class who she did not feel above, yet felt beyond.

I wondered how a woman like her would make love. Did women that refined still enjoy something as inexpensive as sex? Or in her world was sex the most expensive investment of all? Could she be free enough to really let go? Or would she rather keep that sort of thing hidden in a drawer someplace, stored on a shelf? She was married to a man who had access to all the pussy in the world. I wondered how she related to her own.

I watched one of the white executives from the cologne company approach her. She had a different bodyguard with her than the one I'd seen at the hotel. This one was a tall Black man with small twists in his hair.

ALL FALLS DOWN

I went back to the VIP table and found it empty. Only the girl who had been with Milk Adderley was there, sitting alone with the refuse of drinks and napkins strewn across the table like confetti after a parade. The band started again in the dining room. I sat down near the pretty, innocent girl and asked her where Milk was. She looked at me but remained quiet. I asked her again.

"Shit," she replied almost angrily. Her coral lipstick seemed to turn the color of her dress. "Milk told me to keep my ass here."

The way she talked surprised me. The gutter of her voice didn't match the naïveté of her face.

"I don't know where he is," she said vehemently. "That nigga be in and out of here like he a fuckin' secret agent. He ain't sat still all night!"

It was crazy the way her speech was bumping heads with her appearance.

"Ellison." I brought my hand up. "Parker."

"Carmen Shelton." We shook. "I know your name is Ellison. I heard Price talkin' 'bout you. You a writer, right?"

"Yeah."

"I'ma singer. Milky is my manager."

I raised an eyebrow. "I didn't know Milk managed singers."

"He don't usually. But he took me on 'cause my family is close to his. He got a lot of connections here and in LA. My family trus' Milky to do me right."

"That's nice." The waitress came to the table with drinks we didn't ask for. "What you sing?" I said.

"You know: R&B. Some Hip-Hop shit. I'm hopin' to get to work with John. Milky got me in the studio right now with some niggas from around my way. West Side. Bangin' niggas. They comin' with that real shit. They on muthafuckin' fire wit—"

"You got a lovely voice," I told her.

The girl looked at me suspiciously. Her mouth opened a centimeter wider.

"Oh," she said thoughtfully. "You a *smart* nigga."

I liked her now. She seemed to relax too, slouching a little in the booth, letting her fingers play lazily with the edge of her martini glass.

"Where you from?" I asked.

"K-Town."

"You sing in any clubs?"

"I'm singin' tonight. Milky promised me." She paused for a moment. "Have you met him?"

"Who?"

"John Forrest."

I grinned. "No. Not yet."

"The first time Milky took me to see him, shit—I fell *the fuck out*. He's beautiful. He's...magic, you know? It's just like in his music—that's him in real life."

"Really?"

"No doubt. If I can get to do something with him, I'ma—I mean, it'll be—"

"—beautiful?" I finished.

Carmen smiled. "No *doubt*."

"Good luck," I said to her. I drank my martini and got up. "If Price comes back here before I see him tell him to find me."

"A'ight," the young girl said. She gave me a wary look, as if she were sad to see me go. I smiled and walked off.

Before I left the VIP room I glanced back at the table and saw Carmen Shelton sitting completely alone, diminutive and fragile as a flame with the glass in front of her half full.

I went looking for Milk Adderley or Price Ingraham and found Sydney instead. She was at the bar in a silvery dress.

"You look good," Sydney said.

"I know. Have you seen your friend since you've been here?"

"Kayla?"

"Yeah."

"A few minutes ago. Then she went somewhere with one of John's people."

I leaned against the bar. We both had our backs to it so that we could see the rest of the room.

"How's it going with her?"

"With Mrs. Forrest? Fine," I said. "Are you relieved?"

Sydney frowned a little. "I wanted to talk about what I said before."

"I don't know if there's anything to say. Besides, I need to find Kayla."

Sydney whispered: "Do you think she'll give you the disc?"

"I don't know. She's scared."

The band started into an instrumental of one of John Forrest's old songs.

"She doesn't trust anyone," Sydney said. "At least not any of the people she's with."

"Those are all her husband's people," I replied. "She's right not to trust them."

"Have you thought about the fact that it may have been one of her husband's people who sent her that disc?"

I smiled at Syd. "You are smart, aren't you?"

She gave me an answer but I didn't hear her. I'd spotted Milk Adderley, standing alone near the exit doors.

"Wait here for me, Syd. Did you come with people?"

"I don't know where they are. I'll have another drink."

I made my way toward Milk. The big man was standing like he wanted to be alone. I stood next to him and said: "I was wonderin' if we could talk. About a story I'm workin' on." His eyes were fixed on the stage at the other end of the room. Just behind us was a door, a frosted door I hadn't noticed. Outside of it were two bodyguards, one on either side.

Milk answered me. "Cool. After this."

I looked again at the stage and young Carmen Shelton was

ALL FALLS DOWN

there. The mike was adjusted to meet her height and she smiled at the crowd. The red dress was electric on her frame, moving around her like lightning twitching across the belly of a cloud. Milk and I clapped as she began speaking.

"Good eve-nin'," she said. The ghetto-roughness of her speech was made slightly smoother by the purposeful lowering of her voice. "My name is Carmen Shelton. I hope everyone is enjoyin'—"

She spoke for a while and then began to sing. Her voice started off strained, as if she were trying too hard to embellish the notes. But when it eased into something more pure and subtle she had the crowd believing her like every artist should have their audience believe them. She was singing so truthfully that no one could claim that she had no experience with the heartache she spoke of. At certain points she caressed the lyrics and handed them out like gifts she had hand-tailored for the crowd. After that first song, when the people applauded and yelled for more, Carmen laughed. I could see that she was relieved. I was transfixed on her. I could barely stand the thought of not looking at her anymore and going back into my conversation with Milk.

Carmen began singing a new song and I turned to say something to Milk Adderley. He was gone. I had gotten so caught up in the girl's performance that I hadn't noticed him walk away.

I turned toward the frosted door behind me. The bodyguards were no longer there. An instinct drove me toward the door. There was a pale light behind the glass and I could see exaggerated shapes moving in the room. A broad shape—one that looked like a leviathan in shallow water—hovered and then began to move. This shape dwarfed the others. I watched the leviathan in motion, moving gracefully, as if on wheels or wings.

The song coming from the young girl reached a dramatic pause. In the momentary silence I heard a name slip from the other side of the door in front of me.

"*Eva Vaughan—*"

I reached for the knob—hesitated—then the door burst open.

Kayla came out and blew right past me. She was walking so fast she didn't see me. The office door closed before I could look inside and no one else came out of it. I grabbed the knob roughly and tried to turn it but it was locked. I spun around fast and went in the direction Kayla had gone.

Sydney was still standing at the bar.

"What happened?"

"Where's Kayla?"

Sydney pointed. Kayla was talking with a white PR woman. The PR rep was evidently trying to calm her down. A man walked past me and went to them, a man I hadn't seen that night but someone I recognized as being in John Forrest's entourage. He was a young, bald brother with a powerful build. He whispered in Kayla's ear and held her arm in a way that was close to anger.

"What's going on?" Syd asked me.

ALL FALLS DOWN

Kayla took her arm from the bald man. She left him with the PR woman and went through an exit door. I followed her.

I stepped into the hallway and the brighter light hurt my eyes. I saw Kayla at the far end pushing through yet another door. I went through that second door and I was in the art gallery the maitre d' had mentioned before. Kayla was a few feet away, her back toward me. Beautiful artwork was hung everywhere. The music from the dining area was still with us but now it was a low noise being hummed by the faces on the walls.

I touched Kayla's shoulder and heard the click of Sydney's heels behind me. I turned Kayla around. She'd put the aviator shades back on. Tears were pooling behind them. She pulled the lapels of her coat around her so tightly the veins in her hands rose underneath the skin.

"What's wrong?" I said. I sounded strange to myself, talking to her as if she were a child who had suddenly left the playground. "What happened in that room?"

She didn't answer.

"Kayla," I said. "Who's Eva Vaughan?"

Her mouth quivered a little. The lids of her eyes closed slowly and a thick tear seeped from one. When she spoke her voice was full of exhausted fear.

"Take me home."

NINE

We drove down King Drive in Sydney's BMW. I couldn't put them in my car: a superstar's wife and a society queen in an old Honda Civic. So we made it to Sydney's ride in silence, got in, and Bronzeville faded like an old record behind us.

Sydney and Kayla were both in the backseat; Kayla hadn't said a word since we had left the restaurant. Sydney had her arm around her and was talking softly. I was trying my best to think efficiently.

Who was in the room behind the frosted door with Kayla, John Forrest, and maybe Milk Adderley? I didn't recognize the white voice that had said: "Eva Vaughan." It was not the voice of the white man who had called me earlier that night.

I turned west toward Michigan Ave just past the McCormick buildings and noticed a car in the rear view. I only noticed it because it was a unique gray color, like the kind used by car detailers at auto shows. It sparkled in the dark air and the windows looked to be lightly tinted. When it turned behind us I saw the chrome rims reflect streetlight.

I detoured down a side street to test the car trailing us. He followed. Sydney was holding Kayla and looking around suspiciously.

"Where are we going?" she said.

"To Kayla's hotel."

"This way?"

"I think someone's followin' us."

Both Sydney and Kayla looked out the back window.

"Who is that?" Sydney asked.

"He's been behind us since we was on King Drive. Watch."

I went down an alley. I was halfway through it when I saw the gray car enter it cautiously. Then he turned his headlights off. I pulled out of the alley and accelerated.

"Is that your security, Kayla?" As soon as I said it I thought: they wouldn't be driving a gray muscle car.

"No," she answered.

We drove past the skeletons of unfinished skyscrapers in the South Loop. Above each one construction cranes hovered as if they were about to be attached to the moon. We were just outside Printer's Row when I stopped at a traffic light and kept my eyes in the rearview. There was no sign of the gray car. The light turned green and I pressed the accelerator.

Sydney screamed.

The grey car was coming up fast behind us: I couldn't get

up enough speed to get out of its way. I heard the growl of his engine and his tires screech against the pavement. I felt the presence of his car too close to ours; the coming impact made my chest shudder before it really happened. Then there was a slight pause, his car narrowly missed us: he jerked toward the left and went flying past my side. I watched him go half a block and slow down. I started cursing and swung the BMW the other way.

"Oh, my God," Sydney said. Kayla was stone quiet.

We went down Congress to State Street and then farther west. We cut back and passed the Flamingo in front of the federal buildings. Then we hid in the glass shadow of the Harold Washington Library and waited for a moment. I turned around in my seat.

"Has anybody been following you?" I asked Kayla. My voice was rough.

She shook her head.

"How do you know your husband didn't hire someone?"

She said in fragile tone: "No one has been following me."

"Maybe you don't know," I told her.

Sydney put her hand on my arm. "Ellison, let's go."

I drove down Dearborn and over the bridge, into the valley of thin, glossy towers that make up the near-North Side.

"Don't take me to the hotel yet," I heard Kayla say. "I don't want anyone to follow us there."

We drove for another twenty or thirty minutes, fighting the traffic that surrounded the nightclubs and restaurants. I took us

ALL FALLS DOWN

to the beach at the end of Oak Street and parked in an almost empty lot. I got out and looked back. No one else came through the entrance.

Sydney helped Kayla out and the three of us walked toward the promenade. A few old men played chess on the squares that were painted on the steps and a few couples huddled together, looking out at the shore, feeling the warm night and the breeze. Behind all of this the John Hancock and the smaller buildings around it blinked a million white eyes toward the water.

I sat on one of the benches and watched Sydney and Kayla walk to the beach. Sydney's arm was around Kayla's waist. I heard the laughter of one of the old men playing chess. He'd just won.

A half-hour must have passed before Sydney came and sat next to me. Kayla had taken a seat on another bench, her eyes trained on the black nothingness that in the morning would be the horizon.

"Well?" Sydney said.

"Well, what?"

"What are you gonna do?"

I grinned at her. "Ever since you got me involved in this you've been asking me what I'm gonna do. I don't know what I'm gonna do."

"Kayla's scared."

"I noticed."

"She won't say what happened at the party."

"What did she say?"

"She said she wishes she would have never gotten that disc."

A jogger went past us. Her body whispered through the dark.

"I think maybe she should go to the police."

Sydney looked at me incredulously. "And where does that leave you?"

"She got people *followin'* her, Syd. Who knows what her husband and his people said to her tonight? She's scared for a reason. And I think it might be too much for her."

When she spoke, Sydney's voice was strained with both concern and contempt. "Is it too much for *you*, Ellison? This is *your* chance, *your* opportunity. How long have you been waitin' for something like this to happen? How long have you hoped something like this would come along and for once put the ball in your court instead of you having to take whatever job you could get? If you get that disc, baby, you could sell this story to anyone. They'll line up from here to New York to get a taste of what you got to tell. Do you remember how you used to talk about writing for all those mainstream magazines? For the *New York Times, GQ, Esquire,* for everybody who ever turned you down to be *beggin'* for you to do something for them? This is all for that. *This* is the way you get those dreams."

"Those weren't my only dreams, Syd."

Sydney shook her head at me. "What you wanted before,

ALL FALLS DOWN

baby, that was—that was nice, but—reality is different. In reality you need what I need. You need to be above all that."

I narrowed my eyes. "All of what?"

"Let's not get into this now."

"No," I said, "if you've got something to say, say it. Is it something I haven't heard a million times before?"

"No, Ellison. I mean, yes. Yes."

I sighed. I didn't want to go back into the past. I didn't even know if I knew how to get there anymore.

"We're not together, Syd. All those arguments—I know now they weren't always about what we pretended they were about. You got your life now. And I got mine. Ain't no point in makin' each other feel bad."

"I can't watch you be like this, Ellison. I can't." She touched my hand.

"Then close your eyes. You did it before."

"I can't. I don't think I can move on until you do. As long as you're in the same place you were in when we were together, it's like I never left. It's like I'm still there with you."

I looked at Sydney and noticed she was crying.

"Damn. Does it hurt *that* bad?" I asked. "Just looking at me reminds you of how it used to be? It must have been hell for you to drive over to 71st Street the other night. What you want, Sydney? You want to pretend you were never part of my world? You want to pretend you never walked them streets or had to ride that bus?"

73

"Stop it, Ellison. Don't talk to me like that."

I was scared then. Is this what achieving your goals meant? Sydney was as broken by aspiration as I was. The yearning and the reach for it had broken me. She was broken by its achievement, and her need to pretend as if no other life existed before it.

I watched her wipe a tear from her eye before it had a chance to come out. She composed herself and brought her face up to look into mine. "Go talk to Kayla," she said. "She's scared but I think you can get through to her."

"You don't feel bad, about using her?" I asked.

"She's a big girl. She's gonna talk to someone eventually. Why shouldn't I make sure it's you?"

I just sat there, grinning at her.

"I still love you, Ellison. It's just different now. And I want the best for you."

"You told me that when we were together, Sydney. I used to think it was a threat."

I wanted to say more, to get it all out and over with, but Sydney looked hurt and my weakness had always been that I hated hurting her.

"Go talk to Kayla," Sydney said again.

I was about to stand up when an image flashed in my mind.

"What's wrong?"

I thought for a moment without answering her.

ALL FALLS DOWN

"Ellison?"

"I just remembered something about the video."

"What?"

I took Sydney by the hand. We walked toward the Lake and I stood in front of Kayla Forrest. She looked up at me with no emotion in her black eyes. I squatted down and said to her face: "Eva Vaughan is the girl on the video, right? That's her name?"

Kayla said: "Yes."

"Does your husband know that this disc is missing? That someone sent it to you?"

She paused for a long moment and then finally said: "Yes, he knows it's missing. Whoever sent it to me, sent a note to his studio yesterday. They told him that I had the disc and that the police would have it soon."

"He told you this?"

"Tonight. At the party, in that room."

"Who else was in there?"

"Milk Adderley. My husband's agent. And his business manager, Tony DiSalvo."

I knew DiSalvo, had met him at a press junket a few years before.

"Does your husband have any idea who sent this note and the video? Does he think it's this girl, Eva Vaughan?"

"Yes," Kayla answered. "Maybe."

"Which is it?"

Kayla lowered her head. "I don't know."

"What got you so upset tonight? Did Milk and your husband tell you to give up the disc?"

She started to answer but then her face tightened like she was about to cry again.

I looked at Sydney. She sighed and asked Kayla: "Sweetie, what happened in that room?"

"Milk told me—." She hesitated and sucked back a sob. "He told me what he did to that girl!"

I took Kayla's hand. "He tried to kill her didn't he? He had someone burn down her crib."

"Just a warning," Kayla said. "Just a warning not to testify. Not to say anything."

I knew what had really upset her. Milk had only told her about the firebomb his people had used on Eva Vaughan's home to insinuate something to Kayla. He was warning her that if she didn't give them the disc something could happen to her—all it would take is her husband's approval. And although she knew Milk would never threaten her outright, the fact that he could be so dangerously subtle in front of her husband had Kayla shook.

"I want to go home," Kayla said.

I stood up, reached my hand down, and helped her stand. She turned and began walking toward the parking lot. Sydney was next to me.

"What do you think?"

"She's playin' us. Or maybe she doesn't know the whole truth."

"I don't know why she'd play us."

"Neither do I," I told her. "But I think most of the answers are with this girl. This Eva Vaughan."

Sydney nodded. "It doesn't matter. She's gone."

"No," I said. "I know where she is."

"How would you know that?"

We began walking toward the car. The cool breeze had a warm tongue.

"It was on the disc."

TEN

Before I took Kayla home she asked Sydney and me to take her to the Park Hyatt for a drink. We were seated in a secluded corner where there was very little light but I noticed some eyes flickering toward us. And the excitement those eyes offered—their lust, their want, their adherence of attention—turned me on. I liked the notoriety, although I'd always hated to be stared at. But something about being noticed, about being so important in a room that your very presence brought a certain amount of excitement, was powerful. I knew that many of these people knew who Kayla was, had seen her in the papers or on TV, and that little bit of enticement had been enough to make them glance at her now out of the corners of their eyes, like you glance at some incredible thing that's happening just outside the boundaries of your own world.

We had two rounds. Kayla drank hers quickly, and then I dropped both women at the Four Seasons. I asked Sydney to make sure Kayla got upstairs. I gave the valet the key to the BMW and went off toward the subway.

ALL FALLS DOWN

I thought over everything carefully, trying to maintain the same clarity I'd had when I'd entered into all of this. I sketched out a clear path for myself. From Kayla to the disc and now to the girl on the disc: Eva Vaughan. From there the path led to things I tried not to think too much about. If I concentrated too hard on where this path could lead me, instead of following it and navigating it as I went, I was afraid I might wander off it or miss a necessary turn. But as the tunnel lights flashed past the windows of the subway I caught myself thinking of Kayla and her Four Seasons apartment. I thought about having a woman like her, or a half-dozen women like her. I thought about all the time I had spent struggling and what it would be like not to struggle anymore, not have to worry about bills or bill collectors or late rent or no groceries. But most of all I thought about having my face on television. I wondered what the cats in New York would think when they saw me on the morning news. Or how they'd react when my novel was a bestseller. I knew that my phone would be ringing then. Everyone who'd turned me down would be looking me up.

I got off the el in Bronzeville. My mind was full of fantasies.

I found my car where I'd left it, drove past Blu 47 and saw the party was still going. Maybe Milk and Price were still inside, but I didn't want to talk to them. Not yet.

The giant video screen had been turned off and a crew was taking it down. A crowd still mingled in the streets. I took the detour around them and drove home.

○   ○   ○

I WOKE UP EARLY THE NEXT MORNING and went to court. I was three months behind in rent and my landlord had filed against me. Before I left my apartment I turned on the cable news channel. They were working a story about the John Forrest trial. A female reporter standing in front of the Cook County Courthouse said that the Chicago DA was troubled over the disappearance of his witness. The court had given the People 24 hours to produce the alleged victim. The reporter didn't say anything about the party in Bronzeville. They showed a still shot of John Forrest on stage. I remembered him the night before, the smooth shadow behind the frosted-glass door, and that image and the one on television didn't match. The still photo was not large enough, not cool enough to capture his essence. His shadow seemed more authentic.

I decided to see Pablo Dorsey before going to court. When I got to the hospital they were getting him ready for surgery.

"I thought you said no more cuttin'?" I asked him.

He was terrible to look at. It was as if the bed was swallowing him.

"Can' do—nuttin'—about it, young blood."

I watched them wheel him away.

I waited for almost two hours. Court was set to start in thirty minutes. They brought Pablo out.

He was grey and looked dead. They left him in a room and told me I could see him for a moment. He didn't move.

ALL FALLS DOWN

"Pablo. I'm here, man."

An instrument next to the bed was flashing a green strobe. I thought about the green curtain in Pablo's room.

"Pablo."

A nurse came in and checked some readings, wrote something down.

"One more minute," she said.

I took Pablo Dorsey's hand. The Artist was barely warm. His skin was rough. I closed my eyes and thought about all the things that skin had been through.

The nurse came back in.

"What's the doctor say?" I asked her.

"You'll have to speak to him."

I left the room and went downstairs. I hesitated for a moment in the lobby, then I left the hospital.

I got to court ten minutes late but that was OK. My landlord's lawyer found me and asked me my information. When it was my time in front of the judge he asked me if I could pay the full amount due: three months past, plus the current month. I talked for a few minutes but I don't remember what I said. All I remember is the judge telling me I had ten days to come up with the money.

I WAS SICK WHEN I LEFT THE DALEY CENTER. My stomach felt hollow and a craven emotion swept through me and made my skin itch. The afternoon crowds of office workers and Loop dwellers spun around me. Cars honked and I thought they were mad at me. I looked up at the top of the Daley Center and every building around it seemed to be literally piercing the sky, making it bleed.

Ten days.

What the fuck could I do in ten days? Pack.

When I got to my car I saw that the meter had expired. An orange ticket was stuck on the windshield like a nametag. I got in and sat behind the wheel, trying to find some silence. I closed my eyes and saw Pablo Dorsey in his hospital bed with the cancer growing out of his flesh like a weed, splitting open his skin and bloodying his body. I gripped the steering wheel so hard the joints in my fingers started to ache. The scene in the courtroom replayed in my mind. The lawyer, the judge, the jester, the bad acting, the crowd roaring with laughter. The curtain fell. In the next daydream I was evicted. I was moving my things into Pablo Dorsey's room. I was lying in the bed on the other side of the green curtain and I wondered if I had always been there, if I was there when I'd visited Pablo the day before, the hidden man across the room, keeping the curtain drawn because I didn't want to look at myself.

A cab's horn blew me back to wakefulness. I started the car and pulled into traffic. *To hell with this.* I couldn't afford to worry about things I couldn't control. I erased the thoughts of Pablo and the courtroom and everyone I owed or who owed me out of my head and drove to the expressway that would take me to the

ALL FALLS DOWN

West Side. I had to make this happen.

The sky was getting dark over the buildings on Washington Boulevard, but I don't think I even noticed when it started to rain. I took off like a bird somewhere over the Eisenhower, high on adrenaline and fueled by the determination you feel when things have gotten so fucked up you know you're either going to drown, or dare the water to get you wet.

I chose to dare the water. And set out to find Eva Vaughan.

ELEVEN

I went to a corner on the West Side where the street curved a few blocks later into the Garfield Park Conservatory. It had stopped raining. I got out and looked at the building in front of me, the Ashe House, a community center owned and operated by the next-door church, Saint Catherine. The church was Catholic with a Black parish and a white priest. His name was Father Capozziello. He was known all over the West Side as Father Capo. He had been in the news more than once in his twenty-five years as leader of this large parish, usually for his activism, which was always on behalf of the people of his church or the poor folks who lived in the Black neighborhoods that surrounded it. People considered him a saint.

I went to the Ashe House entrance and looked at the emblem that marked the glass doors: an "A" in fancy script with a circle of words surrounding it. The words were Pride, Respect, Honesty, and Faith. I pushed against the glass and went in. Two young girls were sitting behind the front desk giggling.

"I'm looking for Father Capo," I said. "Is he here or next

ALL FALLS DOWN

door?"

"He might be here," one of the girls said. They looked junior high school age. "He usually referees the boys' basketball games in the afternoon."

"My name is Ellison Parker, from *Swish* magazine. Can I go back and see him?"

"Just sign that sheet."

I went through another set of double doors and down a hallway. There were several rooms from which I could hear the sound of instruction, after-school sessions being taught to kids who couldn't afford tutors. In the gymnasium there were seven boys playing ball while several young girls talked on the small set of bleachers that lined the wall. I asked one of the boys about Father Capo.

"He was just here. Said he had to go back to tha' church. You can go out that way and get there through the alley."

I went through the door into a broad alley that cut behind the church on its way to the next street. A white man holding a metal clipboard was reading the gas meter. He wrote the numbers on his clipboard, glanced at me like he was scared, and hurried away. I went down the alley and into the church's rear entrance. I walked past several rooms and a rectory, up a flight of stairs, down one hallway and then another and finally found myself in the sanctuary.

The church ceiling arched in gold undulations and in front of me a tide of crimson benches flowed to the back. The polished brown wood of confessional booths gleamed on the left. Christ soared above and behind me in the pulpit, his arms wide as wings but nailed to the cross. I heard the creak of a door opening and turned to see Father Capo coming out of an exit near the choir stand.

"Can I help you?"

"Father Capozziello," I said, "do you remember me?"

The priest came closer. He was slender, a few inches shorter than I was, with Italian-brown skin and black hair. He wore glasses that gave age to a face that was ageless. I guessed he was about fifty based on the number of years he had served at Saint Catherine, but he looked closer to thirty. I watched his eyes brighten and then go warm.

"Ah, the reporter from the Hip-Hop magazine. From two years ago?"

"Yes. I hope you read the article."

"I did," the priest said. "The story of the 'Italian ghetto priest and his young hoop stars.'"

"We gotta sell the story."

"I understand," he said. "It was very flattering to have my work with the children acknowledged. I believe it brought more kids to God's flock here."

"Can we sit?"

"Of course."

He led the way to a front pew. Before we spoke again I heard the rumble of the Lake Street el a few blocks away.

"I need something, Father. A favor."

ALL FALLS DOWN

"I'm listening," the priest said and smiled.

He was used to people asking him for things. He was one of the most powerful men on the West Side. I imagined that businessmen and politicos had all been religious to his offering plate.

"I need you to vouch for me, Father," I told him. And then I said: "I need you to tell Eva Vaughan it's OK to talk to me."

Capoziello's handsome face became granite. His sensitive brown eyes hardened. The Father looked away from me, trying to compose a response. I reached over and touched his arm.

"Father," I said.

"I don't know—"

"I know she's here, Father. I know you're keeping her."

He just stared at me.

"You're a terrible liar, Father," I said. "It's all in your face."

His features relaxed.

"It's important that I speak to her now. We don't have much time."

He thought for a moment. "How did you know she was here? What do you want with her?"

"People are looking for her."

"This I know."

"They'll find her sooner or later. Let me talk to her first."

The priest rubbed his chin. "What do you have to do with this?"

I told the standard lie that held some truth: "I'm working on a story. I need to talk to her."

"She doesn't want to speak with anyone. Certainly not a reporter."

"Let her decide. After she hears what I got to say. I can keep her safe, Father."

The priest looked at me with some shock. "Are you telling me that someone *is* trying to hurt her?"

"They proved that with the fire."

"And now they're coming after her? Who?"

"Let me talk to her. I'll tell both of you everything."

The priest thought again. "I told her not to go back to court. The police have not guaranteed her safety. And, besides, they'll never convict..." His words faded.

"Not without her," I said.

"Is that why you're here? To convince her to go back to the police?"

"I'm only interested in her life right now, Father. There are other people looking for her, not just the police."

Capo frowned and then looked toward the altar. He was thinking for a long time before he finally got up and stood in front of me.

"I want you to follow me," he said. "And I want you to remember you are in God's house."

I hadn't forgotten that; not during the whole time I'd spent lying to the priest's face.

TWELVE

We went into the rectory, past a sitting area and an office and came finally to a room where there was a glow of light underneath the closed door. The Father looked at me.

"Eva is here," he said. "She came to me after the fire."

I stayed quiet.

"Let me go in first," the priest told me. "To let her know about you and see if she is willing to talk." He knocked softly against the door and then entered.

I looked at a picture tacked to the wall. It was an image of the archangel Michael. In most pictures he is white, but in this picture his skin was the color of caramel candy and his hair was dark brown. His perfect body hovered in the air in front of some normal-looking folk. It was obvious that they loved him; you could see it on every one of their faces.

A few minutes later the priest came out.

"How can we be sure you're not working with the people who are trying to harm her?"

"Does she know who's trying to harm her?"

He looked at me blankly. In the dimness of the hallway all I could see clearly was his face and the white square in the middle of his collar.

"She's only seventeen, Mr. Parker. She's been through a lot. It took courage for her to go to the police. Now she's been forced to leave her home and her family because her life has been put in danger. I cannot be responsible for causing her more harm."

Something occurred to me. "What about her family, Father? Why isn't she with them?"

"Just her mother," Capo answered. "She's afraid that if she goes home her mother could be hurt too."

"Let me talk to her."

The Italian priest did not move. His eyes were searching my face. Perhaps he could see more of me than I could see of him. He opened the door and went inside again.

A few minutes later the door opened for me and I saw Capozziello standing in the center of a small bedroom, motioning me inside. A window high above a dresser, almost to the ceiling, was letting in the bright light that had come after the storm. To my right was a narrow bed with a white-metal headboard that curled into a design similar to a harp. Plump, iron angels had been positioned on either end and a larger angel was mounted at the center. In the middle of the bed a girl with beautiful brown skin and eyes puffy from crying sat still. Her hair was disheveled and fell loosely around an oval face that could have belonged to a woman of twenty-five or a girl as young as sixteen. An iPod glowed by her side. She was sitting on the bed, Indian style, in faded blue jeans with bare feet up under her and a grey sweat jacket over her shoulders. Underneath the jacket she wore a black t-shirt with the word "Pride" written across it and, in tiny print underneath, the name and address of the Ashe House. I noticed the pink ball of tissue in her right hand and the full box next to her on the bed.

"Eva," Father Capo said quietly, "this is Ellison Parker."

The girl looked up at Capo, sniffled, and then turned to me. The plainness of her face was perfect. It needed no make-up, no disguise. By appearance Eva Vaughan seemed void of everything but candor. She was the same girl I had seen on the disc in Kayla Forrest's hotel suite, the same girl who had knowingly or unknowingly looked into the camera and shown the intelligence in her stare.

"Hello, Eva."

She didn't waste any time. "How did you know where I was?"

Her voice ached like a child's, but underneath it was a determined tone.

I took a breath. "I'll explain all of that. For the moment no one else knows you're here. But if I figured it out, so will they."

"Who?" Capo asked.

"I think some people who have a stake in John Forrest's career, some people who don't want to see him go to jail, will try to make sure Eva doesn't go back to the police."

"I'm *not* going back to the police."

"These people will make sure of that."

The priest moved toward me. "You're trying to scare her."

"No. I'm telling her the truth."

Eva started crying. Not heavily. I saw tears slide slowly down her cheek like drops of rain on a window.

"Eva," I said, patiently, "I'm not trying to scare you."

"How did you find me?"

I took a deep breath. Did the priest already know?

"There was a,—" I paused. And then I looked directly in her eyes. "There was a video. A recording."

The girl shook her head at me. I looked at Father Capozziello. His face was serious.

"Explain this, Mr. Parker."

I stayed with the Father. "This girl's problems are more than what you know, Father. Some of what she was involved in, what she *did* with John Forrest—it was captured on a video. The two of them together, sexually. I've seen the disc. Someone is using it to leverage their end in all of this. I don't know who that someone is yet. But I know that this disc will make its way to the media, one way or another. And when that happens, things will get much crazier."

Father Capo stared at me.

I looked at Eva. Her mouth was open. I didn't think she believed me. She stood up.

ALL FALLS DOWN

The girl put her feet into sneakers that were sitting by the bed. She came close to me and her head began to shake, side to side.

"You're lying. There's no video. You're lying."

"There's a disc."

"Shut up. Shut up!"

I said: "Calm down. I'm not lying to you. I've seen it."

Her face became intensely sad. "Oh my God."

"Mr. Parker." Father Capo had recovered from his shock. "Let me see this disc."

"I don't have it."

"Who does?"

"I can't tell you that."

"I was never videotaped," Eva Vaughan was saying. "No one ever videotaped me."

"John Forrest did," I said. "I saw it."

The girl sat on the bed again. Her body hunched over. I looked at the priest.

"It's true, Father. That's how I found her here."

"I don't understand," he said.

"It was on the video. Eva's handbag fell to the floor. An Ashe House visitor's pass had fallen out of the bag with the rest of her stuff. You gave me that same type of pass when I came here to interview you two years ago, Father. Eva must have been here recently. Maybe she was one of the kids who shows up sometimes for your after-school program. The visitor's pass is distinctive. It has that 'A' logo with the words written around it. The DA and the police have searched everywhere anyone has told them Eva might be but no one has thought of the Ashe House because she isn't officially enrolled here. It was the perfect place to hide. I know you, Father Capozziello. You could hide her. You would hide her. I wasn't a hundred percent positive and I didn't know where else to look if I was wrong. But it made sense that Eva would be here."

The Father didn't say anything for a minute. The girl was not moving on the bed. But I knew she had heard me.

"And you think the other people who have seen this video will find her too?"

"It's only a matter of time."

"And what do you propose? That I let you take Eva from here? Where would you take her?"

"Look," I said to both of them, "hiding out is not going to solve anything. If they drop the charges against John Forrest because Eva doesn't show up they'll simply re-file whenever she does. Once they get hold of this disc the DA will subpoena her. Maybe before the disc showed up she could hide from this, but not now. The people who don't want Eva to testify have all the reason in the world to find her now. They'll try to end this for good."

The priest shook his head. When he spoke it was more to himself than to me.

"I want to trust you, Mr. Parker, but first you must understa—"

A voice came from the hall, saying Capozziello's name. He went out. When he stuck his head back in the door he spoke to Eva Vaughan.

"A parishioner needs my assistance. I'll be a few minutes. Will you be OK with Mr. Parker?"

The girl raised her head. She had a tissue in her hand that she used to dry her face. "I'll be OK."

Before he left the priest gave me a look. It was as if I'd just pointed out a typo in the New Testament. The look was a warning meant to make me behave.

I didn't have time to think about Father Capo. I had Eva Vaughan alone for a few minutes and I needed to make her see that I was the way through all of this.

"Eva," I said, sitting next to her, "this can all turn out all right."

She said without looking at me: "You saw a video, a video of me and John together."

I hesitated. I didn't want to get her more upset. "Yeah."

"You saw...me. Do you know who sent it?"

"It doesn't matter. I may be able to convince the person who has it to destroy it."

She looked at me for a moment with hope. And then the old look crept back and covered her face.

"You won't tell me who has it?"

"You didn't know he was recording you?" I asked her.

"No." Something in her voice was too adamant. Suddenly I

was sure that she was lying.

"If you sent this disc, now would be a good time to tell me."

She glared at me with as much hatred as you could have for someone you've only known for ten minutes.

"I didn't send nobody nothin'."

I decided to let it go. "If you come back with me, if you follow through with the charges, there's a good chance he could go to jail."

"No one like him goes to jail."

"It could happen. If you testify."

Eva's eyes were wet and warm. The next question she asked me was honest in its curiosity.

"What do you get out of all this? Why are you here?"

"I get a story out of it. And I get to see the right thing done. I get to know you're safe, and that he's not."

She plucked a tissue from the box and blew her nose. I listened for sounds in the hallway but it was quiet. I wondered where Father Capozziello had gone. I stood up.

"All you want is an interview," Eva said. "You're a reporter."

"I do want an interview. But this is more than a story to me." I was telling the truth.

Eva stood and came toward me. I thought I heard something in the hallway but Father Capozziello still didn't show. Eva was standing close to me, her eyes in my eyes, searching, or

ALL FALLS DOWN

giving me one last chance to be fully honest.

"I don't know what you want from me," she said. Her teeth were clenched and she was shaking, angry and scared at the same time. "I don't know what any of you want from me."

In an impulsive moment I touched her arms, pulled her into me, and held her. She needed a different shoulder to cry on other than the black cloth of the church. She needed a Black shoulder.

The sunlight from the window cut the room in half. Eva's bed was in shadows. We stood in the light. When I think about it now I feel like I should have known something was about to happen. I should have had some sense of it.

A shadow covered the sun. Not a cloud. I looked up.

Before my eyes could focus I heard the crash of the window breaking.

The sound of the shot came at the same time, but for some reason I was more aware of the window exploding. And then came that critical moment when you either freeze up or hit the ground. I'm here now because I hit the ground. I carried Eva Vaughan with me.

THIRTEEN

I heard her scream but I was too shocked to hear it with any understanding. To me Eva Vaughan's scream could have been a "hello." All I could understand—the thing that dominated my mind—was that someone was shooting at us.

We rolled on the floor. I had Eva pinned between my body and the wall. My back was to the window. I held my breath, feeling as if my back were twice as wide as it really was and at any second I expected to feel a bullet dig itself into my flesh.

In the movies people get shot at all the time. It's not like that. I'd been shot at once before, when I was standing next to the wrong person outside of a house party. It was a surreal feeling wrapped up tightly with a naked fear. I'd frozen for a second and then run, sure that I heard another bullet going past me.

Now, at the church, I was just scared. The surrealism had left. I was defenseless, trapped in a small room, trying to protect a young girl, with my back to a gun.

Another shot.

I felt this one hit the floor, not far from where we lay.

Eva said something, a sound gurgled in a separate scream. If we stayed on the floor we would give him another clear shot. I guessed that the angle of the window and its position high on the wall had been the only things that had made him miss so far.

I rolled a little ways from Eva. I didn't look at the window. I grabbed her by the shoulders and pulled her up with me. Her body was rigid. I heard myself yell, "Come on!"

The three or four seconds it took to get to the door, tear it open and get out into the hallway lasted forever. I knew I was going to get shot. It's funny what you think of when that happens: nothing. My mind was as empty and cold and blank as a void. I knew I was moving but, beyond that, the only thing that existed was the door.

In the hallway I called Father Capozziello's name. I held Eva Vaughan's hand and ran toward the steps. When I thought about it later I wondered why I didn't think to hide us somewhere in the sanctuary. But at that moment clarity was a stranger and self-preservation said with urgency: *"Run."*

We burst into the quiet of the sanctuary. I paused at the front doors of the church. My car was at the curb; no other cars were in the street. Eva was breathing hard and crying next to me. She looked around nervously and said, "Where are we going?"

I went down a few steps and looked in both directions. The day was lucid, clear and quiet. All I could hear was the pain of my own breathing.

"This way," I said. We went in the direction of my car.

I saw the grey Cadillac coming around the edge of the block, slowly bending the corner as if it was unsure it was heading in the right direction. It sparkled in the daylight just as it had done the night it had chased Kayla, Sydney and me through the Loop.

"What's wrong?" Eva said. I was backing up. I didn't know if they had seen us behind the Caddy's tinted windows. Then the car sped up. I pulled Eva in the other direction.

"Shit! Come on!"

"What's—"

"*Come on!*"

We ran up the block and cut through an alley. Then down the next block, around the corner, and through a different alley. We went like this until we reached Lake Street. Above our heads the el tracks formed a canopy and around us was a mix of corner stores, carryouts and beauty supply's.

I looked back but didn't see the grey car. I kept hold of Eva while we slowed to a walk and mixed in with the street crowd. I felt her hand gripping mine hard enough that it hurt. She started talking, breathlessly, while we walked.

"Don't you have a cell? We should call the police. Should we go back to the church?"

"The cops should be on their way. Someone at the Ashe House had to hear those shots." But it occurred to me that shots

ALL FALLS DOWN

were common in that neighborhood. How often did they call the cops?

"Father Capo must have heard them," I added.

"Then let's go back. I want Father Capo."

"It ain't safe there. I'll call him once we're a little farther away."

I stopped on a corner. We stood there for a moment and I scanned the street. There was no sign of the grey car. I looked at the faces in the crowd. None of them looked back at me. *But they could be here*, I thought. At any moment: BOOM.

I saw a face that bothered me. He had dark-black skin and thick eyebrows. He looked at me and his eyebrows furrowed. I didn't know if he was mad that I was staring at him or if it was something else. He was walking toward where we stood, a dozen or more feet away. Eva was behind me, my body between the stranger and her. He and I maintained eye contact while he passed. A few feet away from me he said, "What the fuck you lookin' at?"

I didn't answer him and I guess the look in my eyes kept him from stopping.

When the man with the thick eyebrows was gone I looked farther down the block. Three boys were arguing on a corner. Next to them was an old man selling papers and magazines from his stand. He yelled something at the arguing boys and waved a magazine at them.

I saw the smooth grey of the Cadillac eclipse the corner and roll to the stoplight in front of it. I grabbed Eva and pulled her toward the stairs that led to the el platform.

"What happened? What's wrong?"

"We're gonna take the train."

I paid for us at the turnstile and saw the el coming from the west. Eva was asking me questions but I wasn't listening. When the train stopped I pulled her on and found a seat. My heart was pounding against my chest. The train screeched, lurched forward, and I looked at the faces of the people around us. We flew east.

I put my arm around Eva Vaughan. The young girl was staring at me with perfect fear.

"It's all right," I said.

"No. No, it ain't."

I told her, "We'll get downtown and call Father Capo. He's probably called the police by now."

"Maybe they shot him first."

I hadn't thought of that. "It's gonna be all right," I said.

We got off the train at the State Street station. I didn't have a plan. They had followed me to the church; I knew that much. Whoever was in that car had been following me all day. To Pablo's hospital. To court. And then to Eva. Milk's face floated to the shallow end of my mind. I began to form a fragile idea.

"Where're we going?" Eva's voice was dispassionate and tired. I got the sense that she no longer cared where I was taking her.

ALL FALLS DOWN

"Let's get on the 14," I said. "I'll take you to my apartment and we can figure everything out from there."

When she didn't respond I said, "It's safe. It's the only place I can trust right now." That wasn't true. If they had followed me since the morning then they knew where I lived. But it was all I had.

Eva Vaughan and I waited for the 14 on State Street. The day was turning into evening. The windows of Marshall Field's showed a fall scene. Mannequin children played at the feet of a mannequin woman while real leaves fell around them. On a billboard above another building were John Forrest's eyes. It was an advertisement for watches. There were two timepieces in place of his irises, graphically inserted so that they nearly passed as his real eyes. Underneath the picture were the words "Watch Out."

The number 14 came. I found space for us in the rear. We watched downtown recede from the back window like the end of a movie. Once we were on Lake Shore Drive, and the Lake was just a memory of blue, Eva slid close to me and began to cry.

FOURTEEN

My apartment and her didn't go together. I didn't understand why. But I felt it when I opened the door, the contrast of her entering the rooms where I had spent so much time alone. Eva was someone I barely knew but she mysteriously had something to do with all the hours I had spent here, all the work and fantasies that had fought against the walls.

I let her in and stood in the doorway for a moment, wondering about the feeling I had watching her walk to the futon behind the coffee table and sit down. It was as if a family member that I hadn't seen since I was a kid had suddenly shown up in the city and needed a place to stay.

I closed the door and hung up my jacket. I was still full of nervous adrenaline. My back still felt exposed, as naked as the side of a building. Walking to the bathroom I could feel the impact of that bullet hitting the floor behind me in the rectory, the shock of glass shattering. I went to the window in the dining room and closed the blinds. Then I went into the bathroom,

ALL FALLS DOWN

closed the door, and threw cold water on my face.

The voice in my head was saying: *If you can get the girl's story it may be worth more than that interview with Kayla. Or better yet, convince the girl to go back to court; get her story, be the one that "found" her, and* you *become the story.*

I had Eva. I knew where the disc was. Could I convince Milk Adderley not to hurt her? She would never return to court if she thought otherwise, not after today.

I went back out into the front room and found Eva curled up on my couch. Her eyes were dry and the expression on her face was plain. She was staring at a corner of the room away from the television. I sat down next to her, giving her a little space.

"Are you hungry?"

She waited a long time before shaking her head and saying: "No."

"You should eat something."

"I can't. I can't do nothin'."

"I know you're scared—"

She turned the plainness of her face toward me. Her stark brown eyes were dark and hurtful. "You don't know nothin' about me." She raised her chin a little. "You saw a dirty video of me and now you think you know who I am."

"So you do know," I said. She didn't answer.

"I understand that you're scared, Eva. Anybody would be scared in your position."

She looked away from me. "I ain't afraid no more. There ain't nothin' more they can do to me."

I went to the kitchen and came back with water. I made Eva drink some.

"I'm tired," she said.

"You can lay down in the back if you want. I've got to make some phone calls."

She glanced over at my makeshift office: the desk, my tortured computer and a storm of papers and books on the floor.

"Is that where you write?"

"Yeah."

I had a quote taped to the wall behind my desk. It was a lyric from a Common joint:

*They say life is a game/ So I play hard
Writin' for my life/ 'Cause I'm scared of a day job*

Eva got up, went behind the desk, and stood in front of the quote. She read the words out loud then she turned around and looked at me. Her smile spread like syrup.

"Are you still writin' for your life?"

I laughed. "Every day."

She came back to the futon and sat next to me. Her eyes were still dark but they were glazed with a growing interest.

"You believe in what you do?"

"What I 'do'?"

She pointed to pictures I had taped on the walls: Magic,

ALL FALLS DOWN

Marvin, Rakim and more, plus a lot nameless women I had torn from magazines.

"That looks like inspiration. The kind of stuff artists hang on their walls to inspire what they tryin' to do."

I grinned. "You know a lot about art?"

"I write sometimes. I write poems when I'm bored. Or sad."

"You should try writing them when you're happy," I said.

Eva smiled a little. "I do. But I haven't been happy lately."

I nodded my head and let a few moments pass. "You seem older than you are," I told her.

"My grandmother used to say I got an old soul."

"They used to tell me the same thing."

We sat in silence for a little while longer. Eva seemed to be in deep thought about something.

"You know what my favorite thing used to be?" she asked.

"What?"

"I used to like to take my notebook downtown and sit in a park or somewhere where there was a lot of people goin' by. And I'd watch them and make up stories about where they was goin' or where they just come from. And I'd write the stories down and make up conversations they were having with the people they were with. I could spend all day writing about people and makin' up their lives and they'd never know about it. They'd never know I wrote their story and made up who they are."

"Why'd you like to do that?"

A smile started inside of her that eventually found its way

to her lips. "I don't know. I liked the mystery. I liked being the mystery."

"Mystery makes you different," I said. "It makes other people think you've got 'an old soul.'"

Eva's eyes weren't dark anymore. Instead they were vulnerable and warm. "I know," she said. "Sometimes I hate it. Sometimes I want to be more like everyone else, like my friends. Not so serious."

"You shouldn't wish for that. You should be happy to be what you were meant to be."

She paused before speaking again, as if worried she was about to offend me. "Are you happy being who you are?"

"Is this a trick question?"

"Of course not. I can tell some things about you just by bein' in your house. You should be able to tell something about a person if you get to see where they live."

I glanced around. "I didn't know it was that obvious." I tried to make it sound like a joke.

"It is," Eva told me. "It's in your eyes. If a person knows what they're looking for."

I made a sound in my throat and started to get up. "Come on," I said. "You can lay down in the back."

I led Eva into the bedroom and found a blanket. She lay on top of my sheets and I put the blanket across her. She smiled at me as if she were trying to comfort me instead of the other way around. I turned the light off and went to make my calls.

ALL FALLS DOWN

Kayla Forrest picked up the phone on the fifth ring. Her voice was tired. "What time is it?"

"Nighttime," I said. "Listen, I need you to do something."

"What? Wait a minute. What time is it? I've got to be somewhere." She was drunk.

"It's just seven. Can you help me out with somethin'?"

Kayla cleared her throat. "You haven't called since you dropped me and Sydney off last night."

"I've been workin', workin' for you. And I got some information but I don't want to talk about it over the phone. I'll be over there to see you about it later. But right now I need a favor."

"I'm listening."

"I need you to call Milk Adderley and get him to sit down wit' me."

"Why?"

Something about her drinking was irritating me. There should be more to her than that. "I'll tell you when I see you."

"I don't understand." Suddenly the full quality of her voice was there again. It sent a warm chill down my back. "You said you knew Milk. You can call him yourself. I don't want to talk to him, or any of them."

"I got some answers for you, Kayla, some things you don't know about. I just need you to call Milk to make something else happen first, before you and me talk. This whole thing is deeper than you think."

She didn't say anything.

"Kayla."

"All right. I'll call you back."

"Good. He'll pay attention if it comes from you. See if he can meet with me anytime tomorrow. Tell him it's about the disc. Tell him whatever you need to tell him to get him to sit down."

"OK."

"And...tell him the meeting has to be somewhere public."

She paused. "I will."

I called the hospital next. They connected me to Pablo Dorsey's room but there was no answer. I called the desk again and they put me on hold. I waited for ten minutes and hung up.

The phone rang and it was Kayla.

"Milk wants to talk tonight," she said.

"Where?"

"At the restaurant. He said around eight."

One hour. "I'll be there."

"Ellison," Kayla said. "Be careful."

I went into the bedroom. I'd left the blinds parted. Slivers of dark blue cut the walls. Eva was asleep; I could hear the regular sounds of her breathing. I stood by the dresser for a moment and then slid to the floor and sat there.

Did she send the disc?

She had lied to me before.

She made love to him like a grown woman.

Sixteen.

If it became public, too many lives that have lived off of his

ALL FALLS DOWN

life would end.

Too much was at risk.

A lot of people had reasons for that disc never to reach the courtroom or the press. It was in everyone's interest, everyone who made money off the career of the greatest singer in the world, if this all went away.

Did she send it?

She was a pretty soul. The question she'd asked me refrained in my mind. I didn't necessarily see *myself* in her. It was more like we had both been to the same place, some city, or street or house and now we recognized the mark of that place in each other. And I wanted to warn her: take that place and decide if it's really worth all the trouble. Figure out if it will get you through life. You're still so young. You could find a way to be you and not have to starve in the process.

"Are you watching me?"

Eva's voice was cool in the darkness. I couldn't see her face, just her form underneath the blanket and the parts of her hair where the blue light, coming from the window, touched it.

"No," I said. "I was just thinking."

She sat up a little. "About what?"

"About you."

She didn't say anything so I spoke again. "I hope you're gonna do the right thing, Eva."

"And the right thing would be what?"

"I hope you're gonna press charges."

"No one's gonna press charges against him and win."

"That ain't true."

I heard the sound of her laugh crack like a whip from the bed.

"You try to be so....*convincing*," she told me, "but you're not. And do you know why? Because you don't believe what you're saying. They're just words to you."

"I mean everything I say."

"You're lying. I bet you couldn't write the way you talk."

"What does that mean?"

She shook her head slowly. "You're like those people I told you about. The ones I see downtown and make up stories about. Only I'm not writing the words you're saying. Somebody or something else is."

"You think too much, Eva. I'm just giving you my opinion. A young girl in your position—"

"—should beware of the advice of older men. Thanks. I've already learned that lesson."

We were both quiet. Then she looked at me and said: "You're not fooling me."

"I'm not tryin' to fool you. I'm tryin' to help you."

The whip again. "How can you help me? How can you do anything for me? They're tryin' to kill me!"

"The cops can protect you. But you gotta—"

"Fuck the police! The DA. Fuck everybody who think they know what's best for me! All of you want what you want. No one cares what's gonna happen to me afterwards."

"That ain't true, sweetheart."

"Ellison." She talked to me now like I was the child. "You think they gonna convict *John Forrest* just because *I* say so?"

"They'll get more evidence. The DA has a case, Eva. The letters, the jewelry he bought for you—"

"Everything is circumstantial. That's the word they keep using. Circum—stantial. I'm just a lil' Black circumstance that's fuckin' up everybody's day."

I stood up. "Maybe I should let you sleep."

Eva sat up in my bed. "No. Sit back down. Please."

I sat down on the edge of the bed. "You don't have to deal with this alone, Eva. And you can't run to a place where they won't find you. Let me take you to the police. Let me help you."

"See," she said and pointed at my face. "You don't believe yourself."

I grinned and shook my head at her. We were at a stalemate. Eva sighed and then took in a deep breath.

"OK, Ellison, if you're gonna save me, tell me something about yourself. Tell me who you are and why I should trust you."

"There ain't no real reason for you to trust me. You gotta go with your instinct."

Eva studied my face for a minute while she thought about my answer.

"Where're you from?"

"Dayton. Ohio," I said.

"Do you got family here?"

"No."

"So you're alone."

"I didn't say that."

"Then what?"

To this day I don't know what made me tell her. "I have friends. As a matter of fact I have a good friend who's in the hospital now. I saw him this morning before I came to you."

"You've been friends for a long time?"

"Only a couple a' years. But I heard about him a while before that. He's sort of famous."

Eva's tone was commanding. "Tell me about him."

"Well, his name is Pablo. He used to be a ball player and I did a story on him a while ago. A lot of people say he's the best to ever play the game. But he was bigger than the game. That's what the story was about."

"I'd like to read a story like that." She sat there regarding me for another few moments while she thought of her next question. "Did your mother name you after someone in your family?"

"Na," I said. "I got it from the writer."

Eva nodded. "I read *Invisible Man* in advanced lit. Your mother liked him?"

"My grandfather came up with it. He always loved writers."

"Then he should be happy. What about your mom?"

"She thinks I should get a real job."

"Is that what she said?"

"More than once."

"How did that make you feel?"

I actually thought about it for a moment. "Alone."

Eva seemed satisfied in a strange way. "See," she told me. "You know what I'm talking about."

"Father Capo told me you were afraid going home might put your mother in danger."

"Yeah."

"Have you spoken with her?"

Eva turned slightly away from me. "Only once since I left."

"She's gotta be worried about you. You should call her and tell her you're all right."

"I probably should," she replied, half-heartedly.

"Why wouldn't you?"

Eva smiled and looked at me as if we'd known each other for years. "She'd just tell me to get a real job."

I grinned back at her and Eva let out a laugh that was aimed at the pain in both our lives. Her laugh sounded sweet to me. I couldn't help but laugh with her.

"I've got to go out for a while," I said, still smiling, still feeling good.

"Why? Where?"

"I think I know a way I can make things safe for you. But I gotta check it out first."

"Maybe I should go back to Father Capo's."

I felt my insides panic. "Listen, whoever's after you knows that place. It ain't safe to go back."

"I don't wanna be by myself."

I moved some of her hair away from her cheek and left my hand there.

"It's gonna be OK, baby. No one knows you're here."

She looked down as if she was embarrassed.

"I'm only scared when I think about what's already happened. Not what could happen."

"We gonna make sure that nothin' else happens to you."

She lay back down on my bed and I pulled the blanket across her again.

"There's some food in the refrigerator if you get hungry. I'll call to check on you. I'll let it ring once, hang up, and call back."

I started toward the door. "Get some rest."

"I will," Eva said. I watched her close her eyes.

"Ellison?" she called when I was halfway out the room.

"Yeah?"

"Thank you. You saved my life."

I stared at her in the dark. "All I want to do is help you, Eva."

FIFTEEN

Blu 47 was not as crowded as the night before. People were scattered like dust in the dark. A funky love song poured like lava from the speakers.

I walked in determined, my mind focused on the mission but uncertain how I would persuade Milk not to kill Eva Vaughan.

I knew that if Milk and his crew wanted Eva bad enough, once they knew I had her, they could beat her location out of me. I didn't have a gun. The Glock I owned had been sold for rent money the year before. I asked a waitress if Milk was there. She pointed to a table not far from the empty stage and I saw Milk's back, framed between two other men in chairs. On the empty side of the table was a high-backed couch that ran the length of the wall. I was surprised to see Milk and his people sitting with their backs to the door.

When I got close to the table I found out why they weren't worried about the door. Two men came from nowhere and stood on either side of me. They were both the size of small cars. I didn't look into the face of either one.

Milk spoke over his thick shoulder. "That the writer?"

"Yeah," one of the giants said.

"Sit down, man."

I sat across from Milk and the two men next to him. One of them was the thin, ferret-looking cat I'd noticed Milk talking to when I'd first come into Blu the night before. He was chewing on a toothpick, dressed as sharp as he had been the first time I saw him, wearing a midnight blue suit and staring at me with the sort of contempt you give someone who's disappointed you.

The other man was Tony DiSalvo, John Forrest's business manager. He was slightly overweight and had thin black hair and a precisely lined goatee. He was wearing a suit with no tie that was both business casual and business serious. He gave me a sympathetic glance.

Milk looked at me differently. The eyes behind his glasses burrowed through me. "Kayla said you wanted to talk to me." His voice was grave, as if he'd just heard some bad news, or was expecting to give some.

"That's right," I said. "I wanted to talk to you last night but you were busy." My voice sounded too strong, forced. I cleared my throat. "I got a favor to ask you."

"Why should we do shit for *you*, nigga? Don't nobody even know you here." It was the ferret-man. I gave him a hard look. There were guns under his jacket. I couldn't see them but they were in the look he gave back to me.

I decided to aim all my words at Milk.

ALL FALLS DOWN

"You do me this favor, Milk. And I'll do one for you."

The business manager laughed. Nothing about the situation was funny but my audacity evidently amused him.

"Mr. Parker—" he started.

"Why is he here?" I asked Milk, indicating DiSalvo.

"I asked him here."

DiSalvo cocked his head to the side and said smoothly: "I'm here to represent everyone's best interests."

It was my turn to laugh. "You serious?"

"Ellison," Milk said slowly, "why don't you tell me what you think you need."

I sat up a little in the booth. I had to make him want what I had to offer.

"Let me tell you what I can do for you first. I can get you the disc."

No one spoke. The ferret-man stared at me harder.

Milk said thickly: "What disc?"

"I can get you the disc that someone told your friend they sent to his wife. The disc he got the note about. It's real. I've seen it. I can get it and hand it over to you, or to him."

"That ain't worth shit," the ferret-man said. "Unless you got it right here, right now."

Something about his "right now" bothered me.

"Milk?"

"You got this disc?"

"I can get my hands on it," I answered.

"Through Kay-Kay?"

For some reason it surprised me that Kayla had a nickname.

"Yes."

"Why would she give it to you?"

"She asked me to look into some things for her. That's why I was here last night. Once I tell her what I know then she'll hand over the disc. And I'll hand it to you. She doesn't want to do it any other way."

I was spinning a web as I went along, but my basic plan was there. I would tell Kayla that Eva would never admit to mailing that disc but I knew that that's exactly what she had done. Other than John Forrest himself, Eva was most likely the only one with access to it. Kayla would give the disc to me on the promise that I would give it back to her husband and save her the embarrassment of it becoming public but still giving her the chance for divorce. I'd make a copy of the disc for Kayla to secretly keep and one for myself as insurance. Getting the disc back to John Forrest would satisfy Milk and all I would ask from him is Eva's safety. That way she'd be free to return to court with me as her escort, and the world as my witness.

By brokering all their drama I was hoping to buy my dreams. Eva was right when she'd said they'd never convict John Forrest with the evidence they had and her as the only victim. I knew it, she knew it and Milk Adderley knew it too. I was banking on the fact that he would understand killing her wasn't worth it, especially if the damning evidence—the disc—was no longer in play.

ALL FALLS DOWN

Milk put his giant forearms on the table. They were wrapped in a very expensive grey suit. "But it don't do us no good, or you, if you ain't got that disc with you tonight."

"Why?"

"We makin' decisions tonight."

A sick feeling uncoiled in my stomach.

"Let me tell you what I want."

"I don't know if that matters no more."

I kept talking. "I want your word on makin' sure somebody don't get hurt."

The ferret-man laughed. "Who, nigga?"

I made my heart quiet some of the noise it was making in my head.

"I want you to call off whoever you got on that lil' girl."

Milk narrowed his eyes at me, almost as if he didn't know what I was talking about.

"I've talked to her. She's scared. You know and I know her testimony ain't gonna be enough to convict John Forrest. Without that disc he's free. So let her go to court. Let her say whatever the hell she wanna say. I'll give you the disc. You give me your word she stays safe."

"John Forrest has nothing to do with anyone's safety or lack thereof," Tony DiSalvo said. Everyone looked at him. "Whatever deal you're willing to propose, Mr. Parker, should be one of good faith."

There was a momentary pause where no one said anything

and everyone glanced strangely at the business manager. Then the ferret-man leaned across the table, ignoring DiSalvo completely, and picked up where the rest of us had left off. "Man, if you know where that girl is, you gonna tell us. And you gonna get us that disc."

Milk Adderley touched his man's arm. "Bells," he said. Then he looked back at me. "I heard what you got to say, Ellison. And I gotta tell you, playa—it ain't enough."

Before I could process the right question, the wrong one came out my mouth. "Enough for what?"

Milk looked at me strangely. I thought I saw pity in his eyes. "We need that disc, Ellison."

"I told you I could get it for you."

"If we gonna wait we can wait on Kayla herself. She'll hand it over once she stops bein' mad."

"And if she don't stop? If she wants to take this to the max? I'm offerin' you a way to avoid all that. She said she'd work with you, through me."

"You got something else we want," Milk said. "We need to talk to that girl."

"I can do that," I replied, "as long as you guarantee she's safe."

"And let her testify?"

"It won't mean shit, Milk. You know it won't."

"But you get something, right? That's why you're mixed up in this. The girl, or maybe Kayla, done offered you something.

ALL FALLS DOWN

Maybe something you can put in your magazine. Make your name from. Some way you can benefit from this, right?"

"Maybe." There was no sense in lying.

"You shoulda stayed out of this," Milk told me. The tenor in his voice was gone. Only a grave bass remained and it was as if the music being played from the restaurant's speakers had changed to a different song. All I heard was horns when the man called Bells reached into his pocket, took out a silvery .45 and slipped it underneath one of Blu 47's purple napkins. He kept his hand on it. The barrel was pointed toward me. I didn't know what his expression looked like because I couldn't take my eyes away from his hand.

"Ellison," Milk said. His voice was coming from a block away. "El." I pulled my stare away from Bells' hand; each eye felt like a concrete slab. I looked at Milk. He was still sitting across from me even though it seemed like a year had passed since I'd seen him.

"We not gonna shoot up this restaurant," he told me. "But you're gonna get up and we're gonna go out the back. Then you're gonna tell me where that girl is."

I let my eyes flicker around the room. I saw shapes glide past the bar. But it seemed like I was alone in the restaurant with death and his ferret-faced friend.

"Let's go," Milk said.

Tony DiSalvo scooted backwards in his chair. "I'll excuse myself."

"Hold up," someone said. I realized it was me. "Wait."

"Get up," Milk said.

"It don't have to go down like this."

Bells slid words through his teeth. "Shut the fuck up, *nigga*. You heard what he said—get up."

I knew then that it was Bells in the grey Caddy. Him who'd shot at us through the church window. I felt the same mixture of anger and fear.

"Milk, all I need is the girl's safety. She can't do ya'll no harm on the stand."

Milk Adderley looked at me as if I were a stupid child. "What makes you think I got somebody on her?" he said.

Before I could answer the ferret-man took the napkin away from his gun. The silver barrel caught the glare of the candle at the next table. It flickered something of a cool blue light into my eyes.

Then a body was moving toward me. A thick face, a mouth that was too large, and eyes that were intensely dark. She approached the table from behind Milk, Tony DiSalvo, and Bells. When the two men who had come out of nowhere came out of nowhere again, Kayla looked at them with a defiance that dared them to take another step. She kept moving until she was on my side of the table, and sat down next to me.

Bells had put his heat away smoothly. Milk was smiling at Kayla. The business manager sat still. I felt my breath recede like a dead hurricane.

"Kay-Kay," Milk said. "We was just talkin' 'bout you."

"Really?" Kayla's dark voice sounded beautiful. She was beautiful. Sitting close to me she smelt beautiful. I felt her hand touch my thigh and I was smiling at her without realizing it.

"What were you talking about?"

Milk forced a laugh. "It might be better if we call John. We should probably talk about this with him."

"Were you going to call him just now? It didn't look like it. Were you going to bring Ellison to talk with John?"

I noticed that the ferret-man kept his eyes diverted from both Kayla and me. It was her presence that kept him at bay. She represented her husband, and it was clear that neither Bells nor Milk wanted to upset him. Their insinuation toward Kayla's safety the other night was made with John Forrest's approval. Evidently, without him there, Milk understood the need for restraint.

"We came here because Ellison wanted to meet. Maybe he should tell you what he wanted to talk about."

"I already know what he wanted to talk to you about, Milky," Kayla said. "I thought you would listen."

"He was listening," I said. "We were just about to come to an agreement."

Milk Adderley looked at me seriously. "You don't know what you're doin', man."

"We could still make the deal," I said.

"I can't make that deal. It ain't mine to make."

"We're leaving," Kayla said.

"Wait a minute."

"No, Ellison. We're leaving."

She stood up. I got up with her. No one said a damn thing when we walked away from the table.

Kayla held my hand the whole time I led her out of the restaurant, to the elevator, down it and out into the evening air. Her car was parked right there on the curb and we both got in. Her bodyguard was missing. She drove us five blocks and suddenly stopped in front of one of the long rows of Bronzeville graystones. She jumped out of the car and I followed. We were standing on the curb and I was about to ask her what was wrong.

She slapped me hard across the face.

She grabbed me and looked at me with pleading, hurt-filled eyes.

I grabbed her back and kissed her, feeling her tears against my cheek. She tried to pull away from me.

I pulled her closer.

SIXTEEN

The beautiful white rooms looked different now. I felt some form of possession over them. I owned the calm that had come to them and claimed a temporary hold over their mystique. When she and I—the superstar's wife and I—walked into them, I felt different than I had the first time I'd come there.

Downstairs was the Jaguar that had carried us past the blur of downtown lights to the feet of the hotel. We'd gone up to the 64th floor, come into her apartment like we were both coming home, saw the city bleeding in through the windows, and felt each other's presence in that kind of extreme awareness that happens when desire takes your clothes off before you do.

In the car Kayla had told me she was angry at me for putting myself in danger, and that she was angry at the entire world because that's all there seemed to be anymore, the dangerous decision to do something and the dangerous decision not to.

I think she was intrigued by me, by the thought of us, because I was different than the other men who guarded her life.

She wanted me for both my distance from her world and for my envy of it. She knew the secret I had lazily tried to hide—that I wanted her too. It wasn't because I loved her or even wanted to love her. It was because I needed to have her, even if it were only for a small amount of time. I needed to own something as out of my reach as Kayla Forrest.

We left the lights off and let the glow from the buildings outside fill the room. We talked and laughed and had a few drinks. She smiled, stood up, and led me into her bedroom. I watched her walk in front of me, her hips moving underneath her clothes and all the grace and power of that movement turning me on and burning inside me. I imagined my hands touching her waist and the spread of her legs...and the warm feeling of her thighs against my face and her taste on my lips.

Once we were in her room I sat on the bed while Kayla stood between my legs. I took my time taking off her things. She had heavy breasts and I kissed them and cupped them with my hands. I toyed with her nipples, letting my tongue trace a line down to the bottom of the brown circle and then back up to the hard center and sucking that part gently. I massaged her breasts and listened to the sounds she made to see what she liked best.

She lay on the bed and there were blue pillows all around and underneath her. Her long legs moved against each other. I took off my shirt and unbuttoned my pants but left them loose around my hips. Then I spread her legs. I kissed them, starting at the ankle, and went up. Her skin smelled like milk and honey.

ALL FALLS DOWN

I moved my tongue slowly in certain places and flicked it lightly across others. When my face was just above her pussy I kissed it once, paused, and kissed again. When I paused I pulled my face back far enough for her to see me and I let her watch as I licked her taste off my lips slowly and hungrily. Then I lowered my face again and kissed, letting the tip of my tongue be the first thing she felt, and then sliding it inside her steadily, moving it side-to-side as I went, letting her feel every bit of it, until the whole motion ended in a tongue kiss and I felt her thighs press against my cheeks. My tongue moved in strong, hard circles inside her.

Kayla was panting and I felt the muscles in her thighs tighten and then release. I pulled my tongue out of her for a moment while her legs fell cautiously away from my face and then I dove back into her with as much hunger as before, pushing the volume of her moans up higher and higher, sucking and licking her until I felt her hand slip behind my head and her fingers rubbing my hair as her body contorted.

I stopped for a minute, keeping my control, letting my mouth stay near her. I knew she could feel the heat of my breath. I brushed against her with my lips, getting them wet. Kayla sighed heavily and pushed herself toward my face. I brushed against her again. We played this game for a while and then I brought my fingers up to spread her farther apart and, with my forefinger, stroked her most sensitive spot. I followed my touch with a warm kiss that ended in a slow sucking. Kayla moaned louder than she had moaned the entire time I was between her legs, said something I couldn't make out, gripped the back of my head, and arched her back so that her hips thrust forward and more of her was available to my mouth.

I pushed my tongue deep inside of Kayla, as far as it could go, and tried to bring her to climax. I grabbed her thighs with my hands and held them as still as possible so my mouth could do its work. My entire body became so enamored with the sexual energy that I was giving and getting back that I felt outside of myself. Suddenly I was everywhere, in three and four places at once, all over Kayla, kissing her mouth while I tongue-kissed her pussy, climbing on top of her and entering her while I massaged her back, rubbing her breasts while I took her from behind; doing all of this without leaving my position between her legs, pushing her and myself to the point of being undone; to an end that would leave us completely spent and exhausted: demolished by euphoria.

Kayla's right leg lifted around my shoulder and I felt the heel of her foot against my back. "I can't—," she said, "Baby, I can't—"

I licked her.

"*Ohh—*"

I brought my hand up so it touched her breast. I rubbed softly and then squeezed her nipple between my fingers.

"Ah—ahh—"

I put both my hands behind her knees so I could push her

legs into the air. Then I licked her wildly, my hands keeping her legs where they were.

"Oh, baby. *Fuck.* Ellison. Elliso—Oh! *Oh, shit, baby.*"

It was the only thing I could do for her. I didn't want to make love to her, at least not completely. Something inside me, pride maybe, or—more likely—*anger*, kept me from giving my full self to Kayla Forrest. All I wanted was for her to **come**, I wanted her body and her pleasure, given by me and taken away when I was finished. Maybe I would never give it to her again. But all her sighs and moans and the calling of my name: those would be mine forever.

I paused and let Kayla catch her breath. She was trembling. I lowered her legs slowly back onto the bed and once her body was flat again she moved her hips in a grinding motion and turned her head to the side, her eyes closed, air passing her lips and being sucked back in so smoothly that I could tell she was concentrating hard on her breathing. I kissed her belly and pulled myself up to a position that brought my face near hers. She didn't turn to look at me. Instead I felt her left hand stroking the back of my head while her right hand rubbed her breast. There was an almost tangible energy lifting off her skin, spurting up and into the air, soaking the bed. Sex was everything. It was the touch of her fingers on my neck. It was her breathing. It was the grind of her hips, the way they grooved in some sort of sensual postmortem, refusing to let go of the sensation that had turned them on in the first place.

I felt my heart beating hard. Kayla was still deep in her groove. The energy was taking control of me but I was determined to shake off the feeling that we had shared something. I lowered myself again and pulled Kayla's body carefully to the edge of the bed so that I was kneeling in front of her with her back still on the bed and her legs dangling off it. I was aware of my position; I was in a submissive bow. And that pose fed some other need inside me. Giving Kayla head made me feel as if I could control or possess her, but I also felt subjected to her, like I was serving her. I was still the man of lower class, the broke writer, and it felt good when I heard her moan, when she called out the name of a man who literally kneeled in front of her.

I went down on her again, this time knowing exactly what she liked most and what she liked just a little, putting them together until she was rushing hard toward her orgasm. She started to cry loudly, almost sobbing as she came, her body racking wildly in a sensation that overwhelmed both of us. I was breathing fast and heavy, and realized for the first time that I was harder than I had ever been before.

I was careful not to touch Kayla too soon after she'd come, knowing she was too sensitive, but I blew warm breath against her, caressed her hair, and kissed her over and over again on the insides of her thighs. A few minutes later I was massaging her calves and her feet. Then I was lying next to her, my own body undone, but I reached down and felt myself still incredibly hard, wanting the next part but not wanting it at all.

ALL FALLS DOWN

Kayla lay there panting in hard gasps, the tears finally stopping, and her body settling. She turned toward me. When her eyes, still moist, looked into me I felt a surge roll through my body so unexpectedly that it scared me. I felt hollow and full at the same time. Kayla shook her head at me as if she was trying to deny something she had experienced but had not wanted to. In that one instance a feeling of complete understanding passed between us. I knew it and she knew it, but neither one of us wanted it. We could be together. What had just happened was too good to let go of. It was a start of something. We were in that moment of post-sex that you know is perfect like nothing else can be perfect. That moment when making love turns everything else you do into time you waste until you can make love again.

I closed my eyes and when I opened them again I was staring at Kayla's breast. I stayed there for a while. Then I looked up slowly and she was still staring at me. She reached a hand out to touch my face and then rolled toward me so that suddenly she was in my arms and we were holding each other and kissing and clutching one another's bodies so desperately it was as if we were both afraid someone or something was on its way into the room to tear us apart. I felt trapped by the way her body felt against me. I was in that place men go when a woman stops making sense to us. When she looks and feels so good that you can't comprehend how anything could look or feel that good. It's a feeling close to insanity: we have to own our woman, or else we will never be free from her. We have to hurt her first because she'll always have the power to hurt us more.

Kayla reached down and felt how hard I was and started to pull at my pants. I moved so that she could take them off. Then we got underneath the sheets and lay with nearly every inch of our skin touching the others. Neither of us tried to speak. A little while later we fell asleep. An hour or so passed. I woke up and found myself kissing Kayla, and it seemed dream-like, and then I was inside her. We held each other like we had done before, desperate, and we both panted hollow breaths that escaped like ghosts into the room. I came hard, no condom, and filled Kayla up. She held onto me and sighed with as much satisfaction as I had ever heard a woman have.

For a moment, in that time and space, I felt a deep love for Kayla. I felt protective over her. I kissed her on the cheek, a kiss for that moment and the moment in the restaurant, when she had sat down next to me and saved my life.

WHEN KAYLA WAS ASLEEP AGAIN I went to the phone in the front room and called my own number, let it ring once, hung up and dialed again. I felt relieved when Eva picked up.

"I watched the news," she said. "There was nothing about the church. Nothing about us getting shot at."

"It don't matter." I'd made up my mind. "Go to sleep. I'll be there soon and tomorrow I'll take you wherever you want to go."

ALL FALLS DOWN

She was quiet for a moment. "Wherever I want to go?"

"Anywhere."

"You're bein' honest with me, Ellison. I can hear it in your voice."

"I know you can, sweetheart."

"You'll be here soon?"

"Very soon," I said.

"Thank you. Thank you."

I hung up the phone and went to the wall of windows. I smiled as I looked out.

All my dreams were just as large as they were before, but now they were calm, like the skyscrapers that pulsed in the dark.

SEVENTEEN

I woke Kayla a little while later and asked her to take me to my car. We were driving down Michigan Avenue when she missed her turn.

"Where you goin'?"

"What did Milky say to you? What did you go there to talk to him about? What was it that you wanted to tell me?" There was some anger in her voice.

"Milk didn't send you that disc," I said.

"How do you know?"

"I know. Pull over."

We drove a few more blocks, crossed the bridge then kept going.

"Are you gonna pull over?"

She kept driving.

"Look, it's obvious you mad about something that—"

"I'm not mad," she answered. She said the words through her teeth.

I convinced her to park on Columbus and we got out. I

ALL FALLS DOWN

looked at her when we were walking toward Millennium Park. Heavy lids fell almost completely over her eyes and her mouth was bent down at the corners.

"Why'd you come to Blu 47? Where's your bodyguard?"

"I gave him the night off," Kayla said. "I came to the restaurant to find you."

"Why?"

"I knew they were gonna hurt you."

"But you went ahead and set the meeting—?"

"You forced me to, Ellison."

There were some people walking in the garden. We moved past them into an open space and sat on a bench. Behind us the park's giant video screens showed the faces of Chicagoans who had posed for the city's cameras. The light of their images sent a blue shiver down the street.

A fountain poured from the base of the video screens and I could feel the mist touch my face. Kayla was wearing a long dark-green coat. She loosened it and then tied it closer to her body. Her rich clothes, her thick, dignified face, were all sharply defined. I wondered how I looked sitting next to her.

"Milk told me he wanted to speak to the girl," I said.

Kayla looked up at me. "Eva Vaughan?"

"Yeah."

"Why would he ask you that? What made him think you knew where she is?"

"Because I told him I did."

Her eyes narrowed at me. "I don't understand."

"I know where she is. I asked Milk to leave her alone. The cat with him, the one named Bells—he was in that grey Caddy that followed us from Blu last night. He followed me today too. He took a shot at me, Kayla. I didn't see him do it but I know it was him. So I asked Milk to call him off and leave the girl alone."

"But you think Milky *didn't* send me the disc?"

"The girl sent it. She hasn't admitted it, but she sent it because it was the only way she could hurt your husband. She's obviously got more copies but I haven't found out where they are yet."

She brought a hand up and moved some hair away from her face.

"So she's going to testify against John."

"I doubt it," I said. The part about me getting shot at didn't seem to bother her.

"Why? Because Milky wouldn't agree to leave her alone?"

"The DA has some solid evidence. But your husband's got high-price lawyers and the most famous voice in the world. He won't be convicted."

Kayla smiled ruefully. "What makes you think I would approve of there even being a trial?"

"What *would* you approve of? Milk's plan?"

"I didn't say that. I just need to think. I need time to think. I'm so tired and nothing is—nothing seems to—"

ALL FALLS DOWN

She trailed off. She shook her head as if trying to forget something; then she got angry again.

"I shouldn't be in this position. It shouldn't be like this!"

"What shouldn't be like this?"

Kayla looked at me with muted desire. I saw in her glance everything we had done in her hotel together. She was trying to lock it behind a door she regretted opening.

"I wish you wouldn't have made love to me like that," she said.

"It seemed like a good idea at the time," I told her, smiling.

"It was. It was an incredible idea. Too incredible." She touched my cheek. "Ellison."

I kissed her hand. "We could do that again. As much as you want."

"I want it too much."

"Why do you say it like that?"

"Because I can't have it, baby. I can't have it no more."

I took Kayla's hand away from my face. "You can have anything you want, Kayla. You know that. Everyone knows that."

"That's only half true, sweetie. I could have you, but I'd have to give up something else. And that thing is more important to me. That thing makes it impossible for me to have you."

I didn't know how to respond to her.

"You see how it is, Ellison? My world comes with rules too. It has limits, even though it seems limitless. I think I'm like you in some ways. But different." She spoke as if I wasn't sitting there; as if it weren't my pride she was dousing with gasoline and setting on fire.

"But I wish," she continued, "I wish you wouldn't have made me feel that way. I'm never gonna stop thinking about you. I'm never gonna stop wanting to have you."

I smiled and the smile turned into a bitter laugh. "You're all crazy," I said. "Every single one of you." I gave Kayla a serious look. "But I don't regret what we did. I want to go back there now and lay you down again. I want to get inside you again and—"

Kayla was still holding my hand and she squeezed it hard and closed her eyes.

"Don't," she said. "Don't. You're gonna get me wet right here."

"Go back with me," I said. "Forget everything else and let's go back."

"I can't, Ellison. You don't understand."

I let go of her hand. "You're right. I don't understand you or your world. I don't understand any of you."

Kayla came close to me as if to tell me a secret. The pity in her eyes felt like a knife. "It's because you can't be us, Ellison. You don't have the grace I told you about. You don't have the grace to handle this the way it needs to be handled."

She was bringing her hand back up to my face when something stopped her. Someone—a white man with two teenage girls—had recognized Kayla. I heard low voices and John Forrest's name. Then the white man got bold enough to approach us and asked Kayla if she would autograph something. The two teenage girls giggled. I guessed they were the man's daughters. They crowded around Kayla. One of them gave me a sideways glance, trying to figure out who I was and what I was doing with God's wife.

"Thank you so much," the father was saying.

Kayla smiled. "You're so welcome."

"And good luck," he added. That was for her husband.

"Thank you."

"Can you tell your husband," one of the little white girls asked, "that we love him? I have posters of him all over my walls, and my boyfriend—"

"I'll tell him," Kayla said.

"Thank you!"

They went away.

I told Kayla, "Let's go."

She turned back to me. Her heavy mouth frowned and her eyes filled with a darkening mood.

"Baby, you have to understand, I do care for you. That was more than sex, it was—"

"You ain't gotta define it," I said. "Just let it be. It's gone now."

"And it hurts. It's hurtin' where it used to be."

I let out a quick breath. "Decide what you want, Kayla. Because it sounds to me like you can handle that hurt."

Kayla nodded her head. "I got to," she said. "It's who I am."

"And who am I?" I said angrily, the question aimed not at her but at myself. Kayla remained silent.

"Let's go," I told her.

I could tell by the look on her face that she was searching for something to say, something that would make us both feel better.

"And what about Sydney?" she asked, finding another reason to keep us apart. "She's my friend, and you and her were together, you got a past."

"And now you and I got a past. You and Sydney may be different shades of the same woman."

"What does that mean?"

"I don't know," I said.

"Don't be mad, Ellison. I'm mad enough already."

"Really?" I asked. "You don't seem mad."

"I know how to handle it," Kayla said, and I knew that if we were at her hotel or in a restaurant she'd have a drink in her hand, handling things with her unique grace.

"We still have to figure out what to do with that disc," I told her.

"I'm gonna destroy it. I asked you to find out who sent it and you did. I don't want to keep going down this road, Ellison. I want my life back. I want John back. I know he's wrong and I know he'll never stop doing what he does, but I love him and

I need our life together. I don't care about the rest of it anymore."

"And that's it? You just destroy the disc and go back to your normal routine? What about the other copies? What about Milk and your husband? What if they go after that little girl again?"

"Don't put that on John," Kayla said. "If anyone tried to hurt her it was Milk, acting by himself."

"What if that isn't true?"

She grinned evilly at me. "You can't judge me, Ellison. You have your own reasons for being involved in this. Let's just end it now. I appreciate what you've done but it's over."

"I'm sorry to hear that."

I looked around the park and saw the shadows of other people. Kayla and I sat on the bench and I felt something leave me, some fragment of peace I'd gained earlier that night slip away and shatter once it hit the concrete.

Kayla held my hand and stroked my fingers, rubbing the joints. "Thanks for tonight."

"No, thank you," I said. I tried to give her a kind smile but it didn't work out.

She kept hold of my hand. "Don't be mad at me, Ellison. I wasn't lying when I said I care about you. Somehow, from the moment we first met, I knew there was something different about you. I think it was the way you looked, standing there in that black suit looking so cool by the window. And I'll never forget that you risked your life to try an' help me. Even if you did it partly for yourself. You were trying to help me, and I'm gonna help you. I'm gonna give you that interview. I can't tell you everything, but what I'll tell I'll tell to you. Maybe it could be a 'stand by your man' piece. You could write about how John and I overcame all of this and stayed together."

"Fuck you," I said in my mind. But I didn't say it out loud. I was thinking clearly again, gracefully and with great poise. I silently thanked Kayla for that. The need she felt to get back to her life, to get away from the threat of me, had reaffirmed my own needs, my own desire for a different life. Kayla could have loved me but my place in the world scared the shit out of her. She had tasted "us" and the taste was so good she knew she had to run away from it, run back to her own world, run as far as she could get from a man who could give her everything and offer her nothing at all.

Kayla was my mentor.

Through her I learned a special sort of discipline. She was skilled enough to give up the things she wanted and recognize the things she truly needed. I realized that I wanted to save Eva Vaughan. I knew it the moment she'd glanced at the wall of my office and saw things no one else had seen before. Secret things. I felt connected to her in a strange way and that connection made me want to save her and keep her protected.

But my needs were different.

My needs would make me talk Eva into going to the courthouse, into re-entering a drama that I would document faith-

ALL FALLS DOWN

fully. I made a decision then, sitting there in a park named after the turn of a century. Time was inevitable and running past me, leaving me, and I was too sick and too tired of being stagnant. To be what Kayla called "graceful" meant that you grooved with opportunity. You whirled it around and held it close and made it move the way you wanted it to move. And when you're desperate, demoralized by your own frustrations and pain, you become willing to do anything to keep that dance going. You are willing to sell parts of yourself that you barely knew you owned.

"That sounds good," I told Kayla Forrest. "I'd like that interview. But, for real, I'd like to get to my car now. See if it's still there."

A light exploded to my right. I looked and the white man who had asked for Kayla's autograph was holding a camera.

"We'll be in the papers in the morning," I said. The white man smiled helplessly and walked away. When I turned back to Kayla she was examining my face.

"You're not disappointed?" she asked me. "About the disc?"

"I wish you would give it to me. But I understand why you won't."

"You said you know where Eva Vaughan is. Are you gonna try and convince her to give you the copies?"

"Are you worried about that?"

Her face darkened. "No. No. John will have his lawyers settle this. Maybe out of court."

I made my voice cool. "That's smart."

Kayla was suddenly happy. "Let's go see if your car is there." She thought for a moment. "What were you doing out west anyway?"

"Another project," I said, feeling my spirits rise and harden at the same time. "I was working on my own story."

EIGHTEEN

When I slipped out of the Jaguar on the West Side and saw my car, which was sitting right where I had left it that afternoon, I looked back inside Kayla's ride. The soft light of the interior wet her face. She said, "If you need anything, call me."

"I'll be in touch for the interview."

She leaned across the seat, looking up to where I stood outside.

"I wish I..." she started. "I guess it doesn't make any sense to talk about it now. But, when you said—"

I bent down and kissed her lips. I noticed that some kids standing a block away were watching us. Then I closed Kayla's door. "You better go now. I'll call you soon."

She wanted to finish what she had started to say before. But she settled for, "Be careful, Ellison."

"I will."

She gave me another reluctant look and drove away. When she was gone I was alone in my car. I looked at St. Catherine's

Cathedral. Nothing about it seemed to move. I looked at the kids down the block and saw that they were paying me no attention.

WHEN I WALKED IN THE DOOR Eva was standing in front of my television with her arms wrapped tight around her body. The room was dark except for the pale flicker of TV. The expression on her face was full of fear.

"What's wrong?"

I stood next to her and looked at the screen.

It was a cable news network. They were running a loop of John Forrest going in and out of court while a reporter spoke over it.

...whether or not Forrest's accuser surfaces tomorrow is anyone's guess. What is certain is that Judge Rosett has told both sides that charges will be dropped if the alleged victim does not appear in court. Chicago police believe the girl disappeared out of fear for her life following the firebombing of her home. Officials have yet to determine who or what started that fire. If the DA does in fact fail to produce the alleged victim in court tomorrow, this will effectively end a turbulent chapter in the life of the iconic superstar and a case that has kept most of the world entranced since it began last spring. Amazingly, Forrest's popularity has only grown since....

The news only registered partway with me. I was too distracted by Eva to let it sink in. She was shaking now, her feet

ALL FALLS DOWN

close together and her small body like an antenna in a windstorm. I put my hands on her shoulders and gripped them, trying to give her body support.

"Eva. Eva, look at me."

"I just turned the TV on 'cause I couldn't go back to sleep. They still ain't said nothin' 'bout the church, Ellison, but they sayin' this." She kept her eyes on the television the whole time she spoke.

"It's all right."

"No, it's *not*. They're not gonna prosecute him."

"They can't prosecute without someone to say what he did, to give him the chance to face them in court. I thought this is what you wanted? I thought you said people like him don't go to jail?"

Eva looked at me with a mask in place of her face. It was a rigid mask; the ovals of her face were all gone.

"I shouldn't be the one that has to do this."

When I think about that moment now it seems like I never really had a choice, maybe because by the time I got into my car on the West Side I had already made up my mind about what I was going to do. I wasn't so blind that I didn't know what else I could do, but I was too hungry to want to do it.

"It's not fair," I told Eva. "It ain't never fair when one person has to stand up for something that everybody should be standing up for. But this is the way it happens."

She started to cry and put her head against me.

"You had the courage to bring the charges in the first place, to go to the cops. Now you gotta see it through. You gotta go all the way and see this through."

"It was my mother," she said. "She was the one who started this. When she found out—she made me—I, I didn't want—"

"She was tryin' to protect you."

That made her cry harder. "I didn't—. He didn't—."

"Shhh." I had my arms around her and was stroking her hair. "I know. He took advantage. I know you didn't know."

We were quiet for a while until she finished crying.

"They tried to kill us," she said. "Even if I wanted to go back I couldn't."

I took a breath. "I talked to them, Eva. The people who were after you. I talked to them and I got them to back off."

The ovals of her face returned, smudged with wiped tears.

"That's where I went," I said. "Out to find the people who were after you. I got them to agree to leave you alone."

"It was those gangstas he's always with, wasn't it? They burned down my house, didn't they? How did you—"

"That ain't important, baby. You don't need to think about that right now."

Eva looked at me for a while. Then she put her head back on my chest. I turned the TV off and we stood in silence for a few minutes.

"Come with me. Tomorrow."

"I will," I told her.

ALL FALLS DOWN

I tried to think of something that would make her feel better.

"If I could—" I started to say.

"Shhh...," Eva said.

NINETEEN

Pablo Dorsey called. His voicemail was on the phone when I checked it at 4am. But it wasn't him. It was the pretty Latina nurse I'd met outside his room. She was reading a message he'd written because he was too weak to talk for himself.

"He says," the nurse told my voice mail, "that he needs to see you. He wants you to do something for him and he 'ain't gonna ask no otha' muthafucka to do it.' Those are *his* words." She laughed. "So please come see him as soon as you can? He's...doing better. But not too good."

I hung up the phone. I couldn't sleep. Eva was asleep in my room. I'd offered to call her mother, but she had said no. All she wanted was for me to come to the courthouse in the morning. She didn't ask about Father Capo again and I didn't bring him up. I wanted to call him but something about his disappearance at the church bothered me. I wondered if he had anything to do with what had happened. I wondered if Milk Adderley was one of the many people who had contributed to his church. And

ALL FALLS DOWN

when I thought about Milk I thought of how I was going to make sure Eva got police protection after the hearing, since I had lied about Milk promising not to hurt her.

For a moment I felt bad about telling her that. But once she was in front of the cameras, under the cops' care, Milk couldn't hurt her. I just had to keep her safe for one night.

Sydney popped into my mind. I hadn't heard from her since I'd dropped her off at Kayla's hotel. I felt like calling her, and almost did, but then I remembered what she'd said on the beach. I decided it would be better to call her when it was all over, when she could no longer make me feel like I was half of what I was supposed to be.

At 6 o'clock I took a shower. I shaved and spent a long time brushing my hair. I snuck into the bedroom without waking Eva and picked out some clothes. I thought wearing all black would look good on TV.

I decided not to see Pablo Dorsey until later. If I saw him before, I thought I might not be able to do what I needed to do. But the truth is that I just didn't want to feel bad about doing it.

I woke Eva around seven. I found some clothes that Sydney had left in the back of a drawer years ago. Eva fit one of the shirts and, after she'd showered, put it on with the jeans she had worn the day before. When she was done dressing she came out of the bedroom and helped me make breakfast. Eggs, turkey bacon, toast, and cereal. We sat down at my little table and ate together.

We left my building around eight and went through the courtyard. Fall had started. Red and brown leaves lay like bodies on the concrete. I'd parked two blocks away. We walked and looked at the sun slipping in and out of branches above our heads like a spotlight searching for one or for both of us. Neither Eva nor I spoke. In the car the silence was loud until I rolled down the windows and let the new air snap in, making a replacement noise to overcome the one that had been with us all morning.

It took almost an hour to get through traffic and to the courthouse. My heart increased speed every mile until it beat like a foot trying to kick its way out of my chest. I tried not to look at Eva after we left South Shore. I only saw her in my peripheral. We were almost to the courthouse when I saw John Forrest glaring at me from inside a small car. His face was on the cover of a magazine the passenger was holding. He looked at me as if he knew where I was going.

I glanced at Eva. I felt there was a need to say something to prepare us both for what was about to happen, to acknowledge how our lives were about to change. But when I saw her staring out her window, a strange feeling took over me and I reached out to touch her leg.

I said, "Why'd you do it? Why was you with him, Eva?"

A few minutes passed without an answer. I put both my hands on the steering wheel. "You just don't seem like the type. I know everyone loves him, girls your age. But you seem different. Seems like that can't be you."

She spoke the same way I did, as if thinking out loud.

"I wanted to be like the people I write about. The people in the parks, all those strangers I see." Eva turned toward me. "But I wanted someone *else* to write me. I wanted someone else to give me a story and make me different than what I am."

I wanted to say something more but we were there. I could see crowds of people on the sidewalk outside the courthouse, picketing, held back by police barricades. Most of them were John Forrest supporters. They held up signs that proclaimed his innocence and said foul things about the DA. Some of the signs alluded to Eva, but indirectly.

A woman sat on top of the shoulders of a man, screaming accusations that the powers that be were trying to take down another Black man. A white girl sat weeping on the ground, sobbing about the evil that was aimed at John Forrest.

On the other side was a small group of protestors against the star. They were mostly Black with a few white protestors thrown in. I'd heard that when the case was first made public protestors in Moscow had lined the American Embassy, angry about what was happening to John Forrest.

I felt Eva take my hand. We were twenty feet or so from a barricade. A stream of people was being allowed up the steps; it seemed that only the protestors were being kept at a distance. I held Eva's hand tightly and we went through the crowd, her with her head down and mine up. I didn't think that anyone would recognize her. None of these people had probably been allowed in the courthouse the first time she had appeared.

A crowd of reporters and cameras were at the top of the stairs. They mobbed the entrance and I knew that John Forrest and his lawyers must already be inside. I turned around to look at Eva. She looked up at me, her brown face calm and serene. A feeling of intense warmth spread through me and I knew that she had never been fooled by me. She knew who I was all along.

Someone shouted. A reporter had recognized Eva. Suddenly they were all turning toward us, the entire swarm of them shifted like a wave and began to come down the stairs.

Lights flashed so intensely that I had to keep myself from frowning. I kept hold of Eva's hand even when I felt someone trying to pull her away. It was important that they see she was with me. Later the news organizations would blur her face. But they wouldn't blur mine.

WHATHAPPENED?WEREYOUINHIDING?WHOISTHISPERSONWITHYOU?ISITTRUESOMEONECONTACTEDYOUABOUTACIVILJUDGEMENT?WHYHAVENTYOUAPPEAREDINCOURTUNTILNOW?AREYOUHERETODROPTHECHARGESORCONTINUEPURSUINGTHEM?MISSISTHISYOURBOYFRIEND?DOESTHEDISTRICTATTORNEYKNOWYOURECOMINGTODAY?HAVEYOUSPOKENWITHTHEACCUSEDSINCEYOUDISAPPEARED?SIRCANWEGETASTATEMENTFROMYOU?WHOAREYOU?HOWDIDYOUCO

ALL FALLS DOWN

METOKNOWTHEVICTIM?DIDYOUHELPHERHIDE
FROMPOLICE?AREYOUANASSOCIATEOFJOHNFO
RRESTS?WILLYOUSETTLEOUTOFCOURTMISS?DO
YOUHAVENEWPROOFFORTHEDASOFFICE?ISTHA
TWHYYOUREHERE?DIDYOUFEARFORYOURSAFE
TY?HASTHECPDOFFEREDYOUANYKINDOFASSUR
ANCESINRETURNFORYOURAPPEARANCEHERET
ODAY?CANYOUTELLUSEXACTLYWHEREYOUWER
EOVERTHEPASTFOURWEEKS?WHATMADEYOUD
ECIDETORESURFACEMISS?DOESTHISMANNEXT
TOYOUHAVEANYTHINGTODOWITHYOURREAPP
EARANCE?ISTHEREANYTRUTHTOTHERUMORTH
ATYOUHAVEDATEDOTHERSINGERSANDRAPPERS
?ATTHETIMEOFTHEALLEGEDINCIDENTWITHJO
HNFORRESTWEREYOUORWEREYOUNOTINPOSS
ESSIONOFANILLEGALID?HOWLONGHAVEYOUKN
OWNTHISMAN?WHOISHE?WHOISHE?WHOISHE?
WHO

TWENTY

An assistant with the DA's office tore through the melee and took us away. We went past the reporters and into the building to a secluded room.

My blood was on fire.

I wanted to leap down those halls. To kick and yell. The adrenaline was crushing through my body so hard I could barely stand. My legs shook, my arms were weak. I heard the cries of the press come down the hall into the little room.

The assistant, a small man with red hair, was shaking his head at us.

"I can't believe you're here!" he told Eva. "We just assumed, I mean, we thought, that you weren't coming back."

Eva sat down and asked for water.

"Of course," the assistant said before leaving. "And Brian will be in soon." Executive Assistant District Attorney Brian Downey was the lawyer pursuing the case. He'd tried to prosecute Forrest on another statutory case years before but had failed. Now he was coming at the star with a vengeance.

ALL FALLS DOWN

Eva and I were alone for a moment.

"You know, when you let go of my hand out there, I didn't want you to," she said. "I was gonna change my mind about this. But I saw that look in your eyes. I saw what this means to you."

"It means that—"

"Don't say it," she interrupted. "I know what it means."

The door opened again and the assistant, ADA Brian Downey, and two other lawyers came in. Downey and Eva exchanged hellos and talked one-on-one for a moment. Then he looked at me and extended his hand.

"Ellison Parker," I said. The ADA's hand was cold.

"Brian Downey. Thanks for helping our Eva here."

"I hope we're in time?"

"Perfectly on time. We start in about five minutes. I was sure the judge was going to throw out the case."

"You need prep time?"

"Of course. Thank you for understanding. I need Eva alone for a few minutes. We of course need to talk to you also, in detail." He looked at the redhead. "Maybe we can get Ellison a seat in the gallery?"

"That's OK, Brian," I said, using his first name because he had used mine. "I'll wait outside."

We all stood up except for Eva. "You can wait in another room, Ellison. But I have to ask that you don't speak with the press until we talk first. Please."

"I understand," I said.

I patted Eva's hands and told her I would be outside. I remembered Father Capo reassuring her the same way the day before.

"Remember, Mr. Parker," Downey said. "Let's hold off on the media."

None of the attorneys left the room. I went out into the hallway. I could see the press, like wolves who had been deceived, standing behind a barricade.

I walked straight to them.

THE CAMERAS PIVOTED TOWARD ME and suddenly I was standing in the center of a horde of microphones. I recognized some of the faces behind the cameras and notepads. None of them knew who I was of course, not even after I'd told them my name.

"What's your connection to the accuser, Mr. Parker?" It was the lead field reporter from one of the evening shows. His hair looked brittle and his face was red, just like it was on television.

I cleared my throat and prepared to put my plan into action: not too much information yet. I needed to tantalize them without giving them the full story.

"I'm a journalist working on a story. I came into contact with the accuser while I was compiling information for my piece."

A woman said, "What news organization are you with, sir,

and can you be more specific about the story you're working on?"

"I'm a freelance writer. I can't disclose at this moment what kind of story I'm working on."

A male reporter from one of the cable networks asked, "Where did you *find* the alleged victim and how did you convince her to come *back* to court?"

"I can't say at the moment—"

"Could you please speak up, sir!"

"I said, I can't say at this time where I found her. But since she's been with me I've continued to pursue my investigation while making sure she was safe. I'll be willing to talk about my story soon."

A female started to ask, "How long has the—"

But a man cut her off and said, "What is your relationship to the alleged, sir? Are you personally connected to her or her family?"

"I have no prior relationship with the alleged. As I said before, I only located her recently. I don't know her family."

"Has the girl told you anything about this case or her relationship with John Forrest?"

"Like I said: I'll tell my story soon."

I started to move away. The reporters began to shout and more pictures were taken. I drifted outside the barricade again, walked to the restrooms, and splashed cold water on my face. I looked into the mirror for a while, watching the drops of water on my skin and staring into my own eyes.

I thought about going into the courtroom but instead I went back to the room the lawyers had taken us to earlier. I sat down at the table and thought. I could barely keep my smile from cracking my face apart. But I wasn't happy. I was something more. I was *brand new*. I laughed a little and it sounded strange in the empty room.

A short while later the door opened and the ADA poured in with his assistants, without Eva.

"Is there a problem?" I asked.

"Not at all," the ADA said. "Everything went very well."

"That was a quick hearing."

"It's fairly routine. The judge needed information to determine if the case should proceed. We meet again on the 7th."

"Where's Eva?"

"With the police. They had some questions. Plus we've got to get her set up for protective custody."

"Good." I thought about John Forrest. "Has he left yet?"

The lawyer didn't skip a beat. "Forrest? He's here. They were about to bring him through the front again. They like to show him off."

"I should speak to Eva."

Downey raised his hand. He had sat down across from me. "I need to talk to you first."

"Go ahead."

He took out a pad. The other lawyers sat and did the same.

ALL FALLS DOWN

"How do you know Eva?"

"I don't. She was staying at Father Capo's place. I went and got her." I assumed Eva had already told them this. "Matter o' fact, you may want to check on Capo. We got shot at in that church and I haven't heard anything about him since."

"Do you know who the shooter was?"

"No."

"Has anyone done anything since?"

"Since the other day? No."

He scribbled something down.

"I apologize for this. We're just trying to get an accurate picture."

"I understand," I told the attorney.

"Why didn't you bring Eva to the police once you found her? By that I mean, once you fled from the church."

"She didn't want that. I couldn't force her. I took her where I knew she'd be safe."

"To your home?"

I didn't answer.

"I guess what I'm trying to figure out, Ellison, is where you come into all of this. You haven't told us yet how you found Eva. You haven't said what led you to look for her. As you know, her house was firebombed."

"Firebombed?" I said. "Is that what the cops say?"

"Yes," he answered. He had that irritation in his voice a lot of powerful white people have when someone young and Black questions them. "It was a firebomb. Thrown through a back window. Do you know anything about it?"

"This an interrogation?"

The ADA leaned back in his seat and looked at an assistant uncomfortably. Then he leveled emotionless eyes at me. "I need to know everything you know."

"You know a lot," I told him.

"What's your connection to Hollis Adderley?"

I'd been waiting for that.

"I heard of him. I didn't know his real name though."

"You had dinner with him yesterday evening, correct?"

"That's right."

The DA looked at me expectantly.

"Ask a question," I said.

"Where else were you last night while Eva was in your home?"

My voice was calm. "Handling some business."

"Mr. Parker—"

"I brought her back," I interrupted. "Your case was about to be kicked out, and I brought her *back*. I didn't have anything to do with her disappearin' or what happened to her house. I can tell you that. But I won't tell you what story I was working on or who I was working for. I won't tell you how I found Eva. You got her back and your case goes on. That's gonna have to be enough for now."

"We need to know what Adderley has to do with all this.

ALL FALLS DOWN

He's a close friend of Mr. Forrest and—"

"Everyone knows that. Besides, if you know I had dinner with him last night that means you have someone on him."

"—and he's a narcotics dealer. He may have a connection to the firebombing. And if that's true and you know something about that—"

"I don't know anything about that," I said.

"Where is Father Capo?"

"I told you: you should send the police to find him. Make sure he's all right."

"I could subpoena you, Mr. Parker. If I think you know anything relevant to the case. If that's how you want to play it."

"Of course you can. But you won't do that. And not just because I'm a member of the press. The truth is that you don't know if I know anything. You're guessing. And right now you've got a superstar to nail to a cross, so why not concentrate on that? Whatever I could tell you won't help you win this case. I've done the best thing I could do for you, that anybody could do for you. Be happy with that."

A thin, quirky smile was about to form on Downey's lips. Then the door knocked and cracked open. A young man, maybe a clerk, with curly jet-black hair stuck his head in. Downey motioned for him. The clerk whispered in the ADA's ear, looked at me, and left as quickly as he'd come.

Downey gazed at me insouciantly. "You talked to the press."

"Of course."

He nodded and said, "It's clearer now."

I stood up and straightened my clothes. "I'll be in touch. Call me if you need to." I said my number out loud. He asked for my cell.

I wanted to see Eva but I knew that it would be impossible. The police had her hemmed up in another room trying to decide what to do with her.

There was no one in the hallway. That was my first indication that John Forrest had already left the building. I walked through the front doors of the courthouse to see if I could get to him before he was gone.

I stood at the top of the courthouse steps and looked down. A black SUV was surrounded by the media. It sped away while reporters yelled questions after it. I wondered what he was thinking, sitting in the back of that truck. I wondered if anybody had told him my name yet.

The reporters at the curb turned and noticed me. I walked down the steps slowly, giving them a chance to climb. The lights of their cameras froze. I kept my head low, showing that I didn't want to answer any more questions. But then I raised it, to let them see me, to let all of them see me.

TWENTYONE

I made it back to my apartment an hour later and turned on the computer in my office. The message light on the phone was blinking fast and red. Before I could pick it up, it rang and my agent was on the other end.

"What the fuck is going on?"

Marie was a very eloquent and very elegant Italian woman who had tried to sell my first book. From the moment I'd sent her my work she praised it and she'd supported my failed novel faithfully. She cursed harder than I did when she got excited.

"What do you mean?"

"What do I *mean*? I mean: what the *fuck* is going on? I get a call from someone telling me to turn the TV on. I go down the fucking hall, and see you on CN-*fucking*-N. When did all of this happen?"

"This morning." I was smiling.

"You brought that girl to the courthouse? How are you involved in this, Ellison?"

"It's a long story. But we're gonna get to that."

"'We're going to get to that'?" Marie said, her voice slowing. "Do you realize what's happening?"

"Yeah, I do."

"This is everywhere! It'll be in every paper, it'll be—"

I could hear Marie breathing.

"How did I look?"

I could feel her smile. "Beautiful."

"Good. Your phone should be ringing soon. I think we should—" My line clicked. "Hold on, Marie."

It was Bruce Cohn, my publisher at *Swish*. I told Marie I'd call her back.

"What the fuck?" Bruce said.

"I know," I said. "Crazy, ain't it?"

"Dude, you're on every fuckin' station. You're all over ESPN. And everybody's been callin' here."

"Who called?"

"*Everyone*. Why didn't you tell me about this?"

That was his way of asking who I was writing for. My contract with *Swish* was not exclusive, but it was an unspoken promise that I wouldn't write any similar content for a competing magazine. He knew *he* hadn't assigned me a feature on John Forrest.

"I've been working on a Forrest piece for a while. I sort of stumbled on all of this."

"What's the piece for?"

"I can't tell you that."

ALL FALLS DOWN

"Look," Cohn said smoothly. He must have felt the money slipping out of his hands. "You write for us, right?"

"We ain't exclusive, B. You know that."

"We've had a long relationship."

"Pretty long. Pretty one-sided."

"I think we've been fair to each other."

"Not exactly. But that ain't the issue. You can't afford the story."

"What does that mean?"

"It means I'm selling this one," I told him. "I'm not giving it to *Swish* for the change you pay me. It wasn't assigned by you so I own it."

"Is that the way—"

"Let's save some time, Bruce. You've been getting good stories from me for years. I've had to fight with you for everything I've ever gotten from this magazine. I got to fight just to get you on the phone. Now you're blowin' up my line and demanding I give you a story you got no rights to? Fuck that."

"I've always listened to your suggestions, El."

"You run an urban culture magazine with pages full of nothin' but Black faces. Meanwhile, I'm the only Black face on the masthead."

"That's something we tried to fix. We interviewed a lot of Black writers, but none of them were as good as you."

"Do you know how that sounds? When you hired Mike, or Steve, or any white writers, do you only do so if they can write as good as me?"

"Dude—listen, what I'm saying is—"

"That's just it, Bruce; you ain't sayin' nothing." I hung up the phone.

I went into the kitchen to calm down. While I was drinking some water the phone rang again. It was a producer from the Channel 12 morning show.

"Mr. Parker," the producer said, "can you hold to talk to Tamara Hill?"

Tamara Hill was the morning news anchor. A few moments later she picked up and we spoke for five minutes. Then she sent me back to the producer who had called. The producer scheduled everything. I was to be on the morning show the next day.

I SAT DOWN AT MY DESK to steady my mind and write out a plan. I made notes of everything that had happened that day and up until then and looked them over. Then I wrote out the options I had and how each one could play out. It all looked good on paper, but a lot of it was bullshit. The best way for me to determine how things would play out would be to force them in the direction I needed them to go.

I wondered if Kayla had seen me on the news yet. A brief fantasy blew through my mind where I saw she and I together, free of everything that she said would keep us apart. The image made me feel good but it was chased by the anger I felt the night before at Millennium Park.

ALL FALLS DOWN

My door buzzer rang. It occurred to me that the reporters from the courthouse could have followed me or gotten my address by now. I glanced out the window and only saw one figure, a woman, behind the sidewalk gate. I couldn't see clearly who it was. I didn't use the call button on the speaker. I just buzzed her in.

When I opened my door Sydney came inside. She took a hat off her kinky hair and put it on the rack. I locked the door behind her and then we were standing in my little living room—a place both of us had not stood in together for a long time—staring at each other. A smile cracked across Sydney's face and her cool eyes became wet brown. There was a supreme amount of realization in her stare, as if she had just survived some long journey and was finally victorious, finally able to breathe and be at peace. She held her arms out to me and took me inside a passionate hug. She spoke quietly, but excitedly, directly into my ear: *"You did it!"*

Her arms were tight around my neck.

"I know, I—"

"Ellison," she repeated breathlessly, *"you did it."*

I could feel her body pressed against me. It was rigid, every muscle was tensed as if there was something waiting, needing to be released inside of her. Her lips were close to my ear. A mood that felt as distant and familiar as the sound of an airplane flying thousands of feet above passed through me and forced me to tighten my hold on Sydney. But it was an old mood. It went away, leaving me slightly weaker and maybe even a little sad. But it was gone.

Sydney finally loosened her hold on me and we looked at each other.

"I've been trying to call you all morning," she told me. "Ellison, your face is all over television! *Everyone* is tryin' to find out who you are!"

We sat on the couch. "Aren't you excited?" Sydney said.

I let out an easy laugh. "You got no idea, Syd. Right now I feel...I feel, like I'm floating, like I can barely believe what's happening."

Sydney reached out a hand and touched my face.

"Ellison," she said. "El, I'm so happy for you."

"Thank you," I said. "Thanks...for everything you've done. If it wasn't for you—"

"No." Syd placed her fingers across my lips. "This was you. And you deserve it. Please tell me, tell me you know that you deserve this."

"I deserve it."

That seemed to satisfy Sydney. She smiled as brightly as I had ever seen her smile. I realized that this was as much her moment as it was mine. Something about that irritated me but I was too damn happy to acknowledge it. Sydney kissed me on my cheek and we both sat there grinning as if we'd spent the entire afternoon smoking the best weed anyone had ever had.

I offered Sydney something to drink and we sat together for

ALL FALLS DOWN

a while talking about the day and the future. I didn't tell her all of my plans but I mentioned some. I was still trying to formulate things in my mind.

"What about the disc? What about the man who shot at you?"

"It doesn't matter," I said. "I can't physically take the disc from Kayla. She'll destroy her copy. I don't think Eva would go through with actually sending a copy to the police like she threatened in that note. She's too embarrassed by what's on the disc to risk it going public. And Milk Adderley has to call off his people now. If I got shot up I'm pretty sure he knows the cops would knock on his door first. It's all pretty much in the open now."

"Unbelievable. They were willing to kill somebody behind this."

"You can't be surprised at that. You know these people, you know how they live. They'll do anything to protect that life."

Sydney was staring at the ground. Suddenly I thought of Kayla. I wondered if she had told Sydney about last night.

"What's wrong?"

She looked up and smiled at me with somber happiness. "I'm just glad you're all right. I'm glad you weren't hurt."

We lapsed into a silence. Sydney's phone started buzzing and she took it out to answer some emails. Then I asked her to come with me to the hospital to visit Pablo Dorsey. Before we left my buzzer rang again. And again. It rang three times before

I could get to it. I was about to hit the button but decided to glance outside. There was a mob at the gate. At least twenty reporters crowded the sidewalk, carrying cameras and lights.

"We can't go out the front," I said. Sydney came to the window.

"Oh, shit."

"Let's go out the back. You go out first and pull your car around."

A few minutes later I went out my back door into the alley where Sydney was waiting. I climbed into the black BMW like a fugitive and kept my head low. We drove out of the alley onto the street, past the mob of media at my gate and then onto South Shore Drive. I raised my head a few blocks later and Sydney laughed.

"Look at you!" she screamed. "The superstar."

TWENTYTWO

They'd moved Pablo to a new room. He was alone inside it. Sydney and I sat next to his bed and he laid still, the TV above him on but muted. He was further from death than he had been the last time I'd seen him. I was hopeful that the surgery had been a success.

"Did they get it all?" I asked Pablo when his eyes opened and trained themselves on me. "Did the doctor say he got it all?"

"You gotta go speak to him, young blood." His voice surprised me because it was so strong. He looked at Syd. His eyes focused in scrutiny. "Tasha?"

"No, Pablo," I said. "It's my friend, Sydney. You met her one time before."

"Baby."

Sydney smiled. "I'm glad to hear you're feeling better."

"I'm dyin', Tasha."

My eyes narrowed on the Artist's face. "Pablo—"

"Just 'cause I ain't seen you in years, sweetheart, don't you know Daddy still remember that pretty smile?"

Sydney did the only thing she could do and smiled again. "Baby, I'm so sorry," the Artist went on. "I'm sorry for what I did. I've been prayin' that you would forgive me. Your brother gave up on me. But I knew you'd come back. I knew you wasn't gonna let me die all alone. I told Ellison you was gonna come see me. He didn't believe me but I knew it in my heart."

"You should rest, Pablo. I'm gonna go see the doctor."

"Good," the Artist told me. "I wanna spend some time alone with my daughter. Baby, we got a lot 'a catchin' up to do. I miss you. I'm so sorry, baby. Daddy is so sorry."

"It's OK, Daddy," Sydney said. "Shhh. It's OK." I looked at her. Her expression was soft, and familiar. She was pretty to me in a way that she hadn't been in over a year.

"Baby?"

"I'm here, Daddy. I'm not gonna leave you alone."

"Don't leave me alone." The Artist was crying. "I told Ellison—these white boys gonna kill me if they get the chance. They been tryin' all my life, baby. Ever since I picked up a ball they knew they had to kill a nigga like me. I shoulda been stronger, baby. I gave up for a minute. For a minute. But don't you dare tell nobody that. They come get me tonight if they found out I could give up."

Sydney was leaning toward the bed, stroking Pablo's shaking hand and wiping his tears. He was staring at her intensely.

"Shhh, Daddy. Be quiet now. Don't worry about any of

ALL FALLS DOWN

that. Just rest now."

Pablo smiled. His lips seemed to strain under the effort. His face looked older than I had ever seen it. "I love you, Tasha. Don't you forget that I love you."

"I love you too, Daddy." She stroked his hair.

The Artist closed his eyes, to hide his hurt, not to go to sleep. We sat there for a while and no one spoke. Sydney stopped stroking his hand and then I spoke to him in a quiet tone.

"The nurse said you needed me to do something."

Pablo wet his lips and glanced at me. "Not with my daughter here. You come back without her. I'll tell you what I need."

I didn't speak for a moment but then I said, "All right."

We left. Outside I asked Sydney: "Why'd you play along with him?"

She smiled faintly and stared at the ground. "Because he needed me to."

BY THE TIME I GOT HOME there was only one reporter waiting for me. He was sitting in a van with a camera crew outside the gate. I had Sydney drop me in the alley and I went in my apartment through the back. A neighbor knocked on my door a little while later but I didn't answer. He'd lived across from me for two years and we'd exchanged close to five words.

My voicemail was full. I didn't check any of the messages and called my agent instead to tell her about my morning interview on Channel 12. Marie said nine publishers had called her already. She had conference calls with three of them scheduled for the next afternoon.

I don't know why I didn't call my mother or my father. I was sure one of the messages on the voicemail belonged to them. Maybe I wanted it to be done before I would hear their voices. Maybe I wanted all the evidence gathered, all the dots connected and the proof that I had accomplished what I set out to accomplish in my hands before I spoke to them.

It was hard to sleep that night. I turned on the TV and there I was: walking down the courthouse steps, the reporters' voices loud around me.

That's when I noticed it.

I was smiling.

I hadn't meant to smile, I don't remember smiling. But it was on my lips, at first a trace, and then a curl that threatened to grow rounder. What the fuck? The surrealism of seeing myself on television was still there but after I had spotted the smile it became something else. I felt like I myself was some other person, watching me on TV. For a moment, a brief moment, I was looking at myself as I guessed the world must have been looking at me that night. I felt the same way they probably did, asking the same questions about me. I was unknown to myself in that mysterious way that certain, familiar faces are unknown to people all over the world. I was a celebrity.

I finally went to sleep after listening to CNN describe my afternoon for the twelfth time. My phone rang sometime after

ALL FALLS DOWN

midnight but I didn't even bother to check who it was.

I woke up in the morning and snuck out before the sun rose. I drove myself downtown and parked near the Channel 12 television studio. The producer I had spoken with met me in the lobby and took me upstairs. She chatted excitedly about the "situation" that had taken over my life. She asked me a few questions in the elevator and jotted something down on her clipboard. When we were upstairs she took me to a dressing room and Tamara Hill came in.

Tamara was short and very pretty, with brown skin and a short, stylish haircut. She smelt like a raspberry lotion a woman I had known a long time ago used to wear. She shook my hand and sat down to talk for a moment and was interested in everything I had to say. I was told that we'd do the interview in the 7:42 slot and that it would repeat again at 8:52. I said that sounded great. There was a lot of smiling and innocent joking and small talk. Then there was some conversation of how the interview would go. When Tamara left, the make-up people descended on me and went to work.

At 7:05 the butterflies in my stomach started singing and by 7:30 they were spitting rhymes over the beat of my heart. I had been on TV once before, to talk about an article I'd written, but it was only a three-minute segment and I shared that time with two other guests. This segment of Tamara's show would be completely about me.

I was taken to a set at 7:37 and was placed on an uncomfortable couch. Tamara showed up a moment later and sat opposite me. Behind us a window shown out onto a portion of the skyline. Tamara crossed her legs, smiled and spoke energetically. She could see that I was nervous.

At 7:41 music came from somewhere and producers and technical men started yelling at each other. Tamara settled herself in her chair and seemed to forget I was there. A producer rushed over to tell me which camera to look into. A bright light came on and suddenly the studio disappeared and all I could focus clearly on was Tamara and the space around us. A buzzer sounded, a moment like the pause between lightning and thunder went by, and Tamara began speaking to the camera.

UNLESS YOU'VE BEEN LIVING ON ANOTHER PLANET THIS PAST YEAR, YOU KNOW THAT THE LEGAL PROBLEMS OF MEGA-STAR SINGER JOHN FORREST HAVE DOMINATED THE HEADLINES. FORREST, WHO HAS BEEN ACCUSED OF ENGAGING IN A SEXUAL RELATIONSHIP WITH A CHICAGO HIGH SCHOOL STUDENT, WAS SET TO FACE A COOK COUNTY JUDGE WITH HIS ATTORNEYS AND THE COOK COUNTY DISTRICT ATTORNEY EARLY LAST MONTH. SINCE THEN THE STATE'S KEY WITNESS, THE ALLEGED VICTIM, DISAPPEARED AFTER HER HOUSE CAUGHT ON FIRE DUE TO WHAT AUTHORITIES ARE NOW SAYING WAS AN ACT OF ARSON. BUT AS WE REPORTED YESTERDAY, IN THE MOST SURPRISING TURN THAT HAS TAKEN PLACE IN WHAT HAS CERTAINLY BECOME THE TRIAL OF THE CENTURY, THE ALLEGED VICTIM RETURNED TO THE COURTHOUSE IN THE ELEVENTH HOUR, JUST IN TIME TO KEEP

ALL FALLS DOWN

JUDGE ROSETT FROM THROWING OUT THE FORREST CASE ENTIRELY.

Tamara turned her body toward me to include me in her monologue. My butterflies began tickling my throat.

WITH ME THIS MORNING IS ELLISON PARKER, THE CHICAGO JOURNALIST WHO SOMEHOW LOCATED THIS SIXTEEN-YEAR-OLD YOUNG WOMAN, CONVINCED HER TO RETURN TO THE PUBLIC EYE, AND GOT HER TO YESTERDAY'S COURT PROCEEDINGS SAFELY.

Tamara smiled at me.

I AM SURE YOU HAVE AN INTERESTING STORY TO TELL US.

"I think I do, Tamara." I sounded a little too proper.

FIRST OF ALL, LET ME ASK YOU THIS: SINCE THIS YOUNG WOMAN—AND SINCE SHE IS A MINOR WE WILL OF COURSE NOT BE REVEALING HER NAME OR ANY INFORMATION ABOUT HER DURING THIS INTERVIEW—BUT SINCE THIS YOUNG LADY DISAPPEARED THE POLICE AND THE DA AND OTHER REPORTERS HAVE BEEN LOOKING FOR HER. HOW DID YOU LOCATE HER AND CAN YOU TELL US WHERE SHE WAS HIDING AND WHY?

I cleared my throat and tried to sound more relaxed. "To answer your last question, I think she was hiding because she was afraid. Her house was burned down and I think from the moment that happened she thought her life was in danger. I'm not saying she knew who bombed her house or anything like that. I'm just saying I think she was scared."

HOW DID YOU FIND HER?

"I got a tip, but I can't reveal the source of that tip yet."

I UNDERSTAND THAT YOU'RE A FREELANCER. WAS THIS A STORY YOU WERE WORKING ON, OR—

"Yeah, the whole John Forrest case was something I was working on and preparing an article about. But this took it in another direction."

WAS YOUR TIPSTER SOMEONE CLOSE TO EITHER SIDE OF THE CRIMINAL CASE?

"I can't say that yet."

WELL, THEN LET ME ASK YOU ABOUT WHAT HAPPENED FROM THE MOMENT YOU FOUND THIS YOUNG GIRL. DID YOU TAKE HER IMMEDIATELY TO THE AUTHORITIES?

"No, and that's where everything gets a little complicated. At the point I found her we were both in danger. While I was talking to her about going to the police we were both shot at. I don't know who was doing the shooting. We both ran and my main concern was getting this girl to safety. I got her away from that situation and did what I could to, you know, keep her safe until we could get to the courthouse."

UNBELIEVABLE. HAVE THE POLICE FOUND WHO WAS SHOOTING AT YOU? DID ANYONE WITNESS IT?

"I don't think so, Tamara. I haven't heard anything about it from anyone."

WHY DO YOU THINK SOMEONE WOULD BE WILLING TO KILL YOU OR THE ALLEGED VICTIM?

"I don't know. My only concern was getting us out of there."

ALL FALLS DOWN

AND THIS TOOK PLACE AT THE LOCATION WHERE YOU FOUND THE YOUNG WOMAN?

"Yes."

AND THAT WAS—

"On the West Side. I can't get into specifics."

BUT IT IS TRUE THAT YOU DECIDED NOT TO TAKE HER TO THE POLICE?

"I decided to keep her safe."

THE RAMIFICATIONS BEHIND THIS YOUNG LADY'S APPEARANCE YESTERDAY ARE HUGE. I MEAN, SO MANY PEOPLE ARE CALLING THIS THE TRIAL OF THE CENTURY. I DON'T THINK CELEBRITIES COME ANY BIGGER THAN JOHN FORREST AND EVER SINCE THIS SCANDAL BEGAN IT'S BEEN A MEDIA FRENZY. WHAT MOTIVATED YOU TO CONVINCE THIS YOUNG WOMAN TO RETURN TO THE TRIAL? YOU'RE A REPORTER—YOU COULD HAVE GOTTEN HER STORY AND SOLD IT TO ANYONE AT THIS POINT.

"There's a lot to consider, Tamara. Yes, I am a reporter, but this story is bigger than me, and it's still being written. I'll write my version, of course. And I hope that because of my closeness to the situation my version of the story will be a little more comprehensive. But at that point, with someone shooting at us, and the court date right there in front of us, I thought our safety and her coming testimony were most important."

TALK TO ME ABOUT THAT A LITTLE. I UNDERSTAND THAT THERE WAS BASICALLY A DAY IN BETWEEN THE TIME YOU FOUND THE ALLEGED VICTIM AND THE TIME WHEN YOU SHOWED UP AT

COOK COUNTY. WHAT HAPPENED IN BETWEEN THAT TIME?

"In between—"

NONE OF US CAN IMAGINE HOW THIS YOUNG WOMAN MUST HAVE FELT. WHAT WAS HER STATE OF MIND AT THIS POINT? DID SHE SAY ANYTHING TO YOU ABOUT THE TIME SHE HAD BEEN MISSING?

"Not really. We mainly talked about the case and whether or not she should go back. You would think she'd be frightened, but she's a very strong young woman."

I thought about the conversation Eva and I had had the night before we went to the courthouse and that made me smile. "She's not your average teenager."

WHAT DO YOU MEAN BY THAT?

For a moment I'd forgotten where I was.

"I mean, she's very in tune with what's going on. She understands the position she's in."

I IMAGINE THAT SHE'S COMMITTED TO THIS CASE. BUT THERE WAS A LOT OF HESITATION ON HER PART. SINCE YOU WERE WORKING ON THIS STORY I KNOW YOU'RE AWARE OF ALL THE FACTS INVOLVED AND THE SUPPOSED RELATIONSHIP BETWEEN THIS YOUNG WOMAN AND JOHN FORREST. IS THAT SOMETHING THAT THE TWO OF YOU TALKED ABOUT?

"I'll touch on that in my story."

WHEN CAN WE EXPECT TO SEE YOUR STORY AND WHERE WILL IT BE PUBLISHED?

"I'm working to finish it right now. I'm talking to a few magazine editors."

LET ME ASK YOU: DURING THE TIME YOU WERE BOTH TO-
GETHER, HOW DID YOU PERSUADE THIS GIRL TO GO TO THE
COURTHOUSE? HOW WERE YOU ABLE TO CONVINCE HER?

There was something velvet in Tamara's tone.

"We spoke," I said. I was aware again of the bright light above me. "We talked about the case."

THERE'S ALREADY BEEN SPECULATION ABOUT YOUR IN-
VOLVEMENT WITH THE ALLEGED—

"My 'involvement?'"

HOW CLOSE ARE YOU TO HER TO CONVINCE HER TO DO SOME-
THING THAT OTHER PEOPLE MAY THINK WAS INCREDIBLY DAN-
GEROUS? HER HOUSE WAS FIREBOMBED, HER LIFE MAY ACTU-
ALLY HAVE BEEN IN DANGER...

Tamara's face was comforting, an interviewer's comfort. I could make that face too. But she couldn't hide what was in her eyes.

"I should let the victim speak for herself, whenever she decides to do that."

IT'S STILL ALLEGED, ISN'T IT?

"Alleged victim, I'm sorry."

ARE THE TWO OF YOU CLOSE?

"Yes—we grew close—"

DID SHE STAY AT YOUR OWN HOME OVERNIGHT OR—

"Everything will be in the story I—"

The bright light became all that I saw. Tamara disappeared.

185

I tried to smile but I don't know how that came off. She wrapped up the interview and I was left sitting there, feeling like a naked child. Tamara said something as the lights went away. Something I tend to forget. But I know that it was a question. Her face was bent away from me at first. She was fumbling through the papers in her hands. Set-assistants were approaching and moving around us, getting ready for the next segment. Tamara reached up to her chest and unhooked her microphone.

"Tell me off the record," she said. She finally looked at me. In her eyes I saw what I had seen before: a slightly hidden air of disgust, a judgment of sins I had committed in one way or another.

"Did you fuck that little girl too?"

TWENTYTHREE

I was standing in the dressing room alone. The events of the last week revolved in my mind in a cycle that made me dizzy. An assistant producer knocked on the door and told me I had a call on line twelve. I went over to the dressing table and picked up the phone and pressed the little flashing button. Marie was on the other end.

"How did it go?"

"I mentioned the fact that I was writing a story."

"Good," she said. "I've gotten more calls this morning. Editors of some of the houses saw you on CNN. Ellison, we already have offers."

I sat down. "Who—"

Marie named a famous publishing house. "They offered an initial two-book deal. $250,000 advance on the first book, which would be about your time with this girl and your involvement with the whole case."

"Two-fifty?"

"We're not taking it. That was the lowest offer." Marie laughed and mentioned another house. "They offered us $550,000!"

"What'd you say?"

"Can you be in New York tomorrow?"

"Probably, I mean—"

"Good. I booked you a flight. You're going to be on *Today*." She was still laughing.

"What?"

"The *Today* show. You know, the morning show on—"

"I know what it is, Marie. How—?"

"I wasn't going to wait for them to call us, although they told me I only beat them by half-an-hour! This will drive the offers up, Ellison. *Today* will put you in front of 10 million people."

Marie outlined all the offers that were on the table. Before we hung up she instructed me to get a cell phone before I came to New York.

I had, all at once, a rush, an exhilaration I had never felt before and a sense of numbness and awe, like I'd suddenly been cast alone into space. My heart was beating fast and I think I started to sweat. I looked in the mirror. In my eyes I saw an excited fear along with sweet pleasure, the soaking up of all that was occurring to me, the silly, vulpine sort of joy that happens when—very quickly—you become the center of a universe.

I smiled. And laughed. I laughed like a fool, like I was going insane. $550,000. 500 *fifty- thousand, muthafuckin' dollars*. I rested my chin in my hand and laughed at myself in the mir-

ALL FALLS DOWN

ror until tears started forming in my eyes. That went on for a few minutes—I'd stop and then begin again—then I sighed like you do at the end of a long laugh and felt the emotion slowly go away. There was nothing left to take its place. Suddenly I remembered something. It was Tamara Hill's face looking at me like she was ashamed of me, looking at me like she needed me to right some terrible wrong.

Her face remained in my mind for a moment and then I wiped it away. I climbed back to the hundreds of thousands of dollars that were being produced for me in the offices of would-be exploiters all over the country. Chicago had called, New York had called, and Los Angeles wouldn't be far behind. Why shouldn't I make a movie? Write a screenplay? The smile returned to my face and the curl of my lips felt jagged across my cheeks. Then the door knocked again.

The assistant stuck his head in. "Mr. Parker? You've got another call. Line seven."

I picked up the line. Eva's voice was soft and wet as if she'd been crying so long her thoughts had become permanently drenched.

"I saw you on the news."

I didn't know what to say to her, wondering if she were angry with me.

"I tried to call you at home and leave a message but your voicemail is full. I got the station's number from information. I thought you might still be there."

"I should get a cell."

"Yeah." She laughed a little. She sounded sick.

"Are you OK?"

"No," she said. "I need your help."

"What's wrong?"

"I just...I need your help."

"Where are you?"

"The cops have me in a hotel. I'll be here until it's over with."

"That's probably the best thing for you, Eva."

"No, Ellison." She paused for a moment but I couldn't tell if she was crying. "I need your help!"

"Sweetheart, I done all I can. You gotta be strong now."

"But I don't know. I don't know if—"

"If what, baby?"

She paused for a longer moment and when she came back her tone had changed slightly. Now it was more assertive.

"I don't like what that news lady was trying to say about you. I don't like how she talked."

"What do you mean?"

"Ellison?"

"Yes?"

"I didn't want to sex you that night."

I made a funny sound. "I don't—"

"That night, in your apartment after we left the church. I wasn't trying to have sex with you."

ALL FALLS DOWN

"That would have never happened, Eva."

"I wish it would have," she said. "It's better than what you're doing to me now."

I closed my eyes and exhaled. Eva's anger toward me was the same as Tamara Hill's. I had let both of them down—two women I had known less than two days who had somehow come to expect things of me I had stopped expecting of myself.

"Eva, I know that you—"

"Don't, Ellison. Remember what we both said? We don't have to lie to each other."

"You're right, we don't. I'm trying to build a life, Eva. I'm trying to do some things that will, that'll get me to that next level. Can you understand that?"

"Yeah, I understand. I understood last night. I told you I did."

"But you let me take you to the courthouse anyway."

She was quiet for a minute. Then she said my name.

"Yeah?"

"Do you think, after this is over, we can sit down and talk again, like we did last night? I know it sounds silly but I don't have nobody else to talk to—not in that way."

"Yeah, sweetheart. We'll go somewhere and talk about anything you want."

"Good." She seemed a little happier. "I think I'd better go now."

"But you said you needed my help."

"No, I'ma be OK. There may be one thing you can do, though."

"What?"

She took a breath. "It's my mother. She don't understand everything that's going on. I can't really talk to her right now. But I know if you talked to her you could at least ease her mind about all this. The cops talked to her but they act like they don't want to give her too much information, just enough to say they got her consent. I just want someone I can trust to speak wit' her. I want her to understand."

"I'll talk with her."

Eva gave me an address. "That's my aunt's house. Our house is gone."

"I know," I said. "Eva?"

"Yeah?"

"I gotta ask you a question. Did you take that disc from John's apartment? Did you send it to his wife?"

I heard Eva let out a long breath. When she spoke her voice was heavy with conviction. "Yeah, I took it."

"And you sent it to Kayla?"

She refused to answer me, as if she had admitted enough for one day.

"I should go now."

For some reason I didn't want her to get off the phone.

"Are they treating you right?" I asked.

"The police?" She giggled. "They treating me like a queen

ALL FALLS DOWN

as long as they gettin' what they want out of me. I ain't stupid, Ellison. I know that as soon as this is over ain't nobody gonna care too much about tendin' to my needs."

"That ain't true, Eva. You know you got people who care 'bout you."

She laughed again through her wet voice. "I know you care about me, Ellison. Despite yourself."

I smiled. "I do."

There was a pause and then she said, "I gotta go now."

"Be careful, baby."

"I will."

"Bye, Eva."

More silence, filled with the space of an unasked question. Then, "Bye."

I put on my jacket and left the dressing room. I had a million things to do that day. A million opportunities to pursue. And I had to start writing. I had to have something to show to the publishers to make sure the deal, whichever one I decided to take, wouldn't be held up. Just a touch of a novel, a memoir, an account of my time with Eva Vaughan, the time when I was almost killed, the story of my involvement with the trial of John Forrest.

Outside the studio the street had been littered with wild postings—those poster-sized advertisements of albums or movies you see all over the city. These were for a new John Forrest song. In the ad he was wearing a long black trench coat that fit his body perfectly and shielded the sides of his face with a high, upturned collar. He was walking down an empty street that had just been rained on and the expression on his face was a weary one. The song was called *My Life*. As I stood at the end of the actual street the posters stretched in a line away from me, down several blocks, attached to the sides of buildings and to the base of streetlights. A hundred or more John Forrests walked alongside me.

I got my car out of the parking garage, thought about the rent I still owed to my leasing company when I paid the attendant, thought about the blank checks waiting for me in New York, and felt good. I was almost to Lake Shore Drive when a strange feeling seized me. I felt a wave of panic come over me like I was about to crash into a wall. Suddenly I was turning the car around and driving as fast as I could past the Loop.

I went straight to the hospital.

TWENTYFOUR

The nurse's face looked broken. It was the Latina nurse, the one I had flirted with a few days before. She was coming out of Pablo's room as I was going in. She didn't have to tell me his condition.

I suddenly felt defeated, as if some last fight that I needed to win was finished before I knew it had begun.

When I parted my lips to speak it was as if they had been stapled shut.

"He dead?"

"No," she said.

"What—"

"He had a small stroke last night. They revived him but he's not doing well at all."

She shook her head while she talked, like a child warning another child that they were about to get into trouble. I stepped closer to her, closer to the door, which she seemed to be guarding. She spoke quietly to me.

"I feel silly getting upset like this," she said. "I've had patients die. But I really grew close to Mr. Dorsey. I really like him. There's something special about him."

I smiled at the nurse. There was no one else in the hallway at the moment so I took her hand.

"He is special. Everybody who meets him knows that. It's his blessing and his curse."

I saw in her dark eyes that she didn't know exactly what I meant but that she wanted to know. I could have kissed her or sat her down right there in the hall to tell her the story of Pablo Dorsey, or taken her someplace private. I could have done anything in that one moment because we were bound together by his spell, by all the unsaid things the Artist was. She knew it and I knew it and in that instant it was doing what a star's magic always does: bring strangers together and bind them with a common awe.

"I'm gonna go in," I said.

The Latina nodded her head. "He asked about you."

Her eyes went away from me so I let the rest of her go too. She took a step from the door and we were separate again.

"Tell him I'll be back to check on him and bring him his meds in half an hour."

"I will," I said.

I went inside and saw a shadow across Pablo Dorsey's bed. I thought about opening the blinds but decided not to. Sunlight would have seemed like a sin.

He had lost weight overnight. His skin was gray again. He

watched me come in but didn't say a word. I'd been around dying folks before and you know that they're dying. You can feel it there and inevitable and soon, and there's nothing you can say to stop it. I sat down next to Pablo's bed and kept my mouth shut. We sat like that for ten minutes.

Then the Artist said: "I need your help, young blood." He coughed.

"Anything."

"Get me outta here."

"What?"

"Get me *out* of here."

"You was serious."

"Damn right. Damn..."

"Pablo—"

"Damn right."

I heard someone in the hall and thought it was the nurse. But the sound went away.

"Get me out of here, Ellison." His voice was a hard rasp.

"You don't wanna die here."

"I can't die here. Artist can't die like *this*. I can't let them folks down."

"Who, Pablo?"

The older man swallowed. A lump the size of a golf ball traveled down his neck. "Can't let 'em down."

"Who?"

He turned his head toward me on the pillow. His sad eyes

were milky. "Them people who depend on me, young blood. I can't let them down."

"But they'll know you went strong."

"Not here. I need your help. I can't do it alone. You got to get me outta here, young blood."

"You don't owe nobody nothin', Pablo."

The Artist—so near death I could feel it coming toward me—smiled.

"You wrong, El'son. I owe. That's just the way it is."

I stood up and looked at my watch. The nurse would be back in fifteen minutes. I looked down at Pablo. In the bed he was a sliver of life, the white sheets holding an apparition more than they held a man.

"I know where to go," he said.

I went into the closet and found a tan trench coat. Underneath it was the small bag of belongings Pablo had brought with him when he had checked into the hospital all those weeks ago.

"What else do you want?" I said.

"Nuthin'. I don't need nuthin'."

I pulled the sheets back. Pablo was small and skinny inside a white gown. I took him by the arm to pull him up and it felt like bone. I smelt the stale odor of all the medicine they'd been pumping into him. I managed to get the coat around him and found his pants, some socks and his shoes.

"Wait here a second."

ALL FALLS DOWN

I cracked the door open and peered out. A blood-tech was pushing a cart down the hall. He went into a room and the door closed behind him. Then nothing.

I got Pablo's arm around my shoulder so I could support his weight. We limped out of his room together.

Pablo's eyes squinted under the lights and his mouth opened as if he were in pain. His head went back and he glared up at the ceiling as I moved us along and for a moment I was afraid I had made a mistake. What if he had more time? What if they could help him and he could live a few more months? I'd spent time with Pablo, but never understood him as much as I did at that moment. I decided I was going to get him away from there and to wherever he wanted to go—not only for him, but for the both of us.

I got him down the short end of the hall and to the stairway. I heard the elevator bell make a sound as it reached the floor but I didn't look behind me. I heard her gasp. Once I had the Artist halfway into the stairwell door I turned around.

The Latina nurse had seen us, and her face had gone white. She stood still with both arms at her sides. We made eye contact and an understanding passed between us. A sort of acceptance calmed her features. She nodded slightly, sadly, and I nodded back. Then I took Pablo down the stairs.

I BLENDED IN WITH A CROWD OF PEOPLE in a hallway near the first floor and made my way toward the rear. I went through a door marked "Restricted" with Pablo still limping and coughing heavily beside me.

"Hold on," I was saying. "There's security at the front. They'll know you shouldn't be leaving."

We went through a linen room. Behind some enormous machines workers were emptying vats of clothing. I leaned Pablo against a wall and we hid as two men wearing green jumpsuits went past. When I thought it was safe I put Pablo's arm around me again and searched for a way out. In the third room I could see the rear loading dock through the window of a door. I took Pablo that way and there were a few trucks and men working on them to our right. One of them saw me, thought about approaching me, then shook his head and decided it wasn't worth the trouble.

We went down a flight of iron steps and were outside. Pablo coughed and made soft murmuring sounds.

"Where?" I asked. I put my ear near his lips. He told me where he wanted to go.

It took ten minutes to walk the two blocks to my car. I got the Artist in the passenger seat and leaned it back so that he was lying down. He was coughing less now but had started to moan. I could only imagine what part of his life he was revisiting.

"Hold on, Pablo."

I drove south. It was late morning so there wasn't much traffic. I cut over to Drexel Boulevard and a while later we parked on 50th, in front of a playground that stood there as if it were waiting for us.

    I looked down at the Artist. He seemed asleep. I reached my hand out, and then pulled it back. I thought for a moment that I had failed him; that I had let him die in the car.

    He coughed and some blood slipped from the left side of his mouth. I got out of the car and went around to his side. I wiped the blood and pulled him up gently.

    "We here, Pablo. We here, man."

    His eyes were closed but he moved. I helped him limp to the playground.

    The court was beautiful. On the brick wall that stood behind it was a mural. A giant jazzman played in the center; his blues had affected his skin. A little boy the color of maple syrup sat in his mother's lap. To the right, above more images, were the words: "Feed Your Child the Truth."

    There were two kids shooting around at the basket nearest the street. Pablo stopped me for a second and lifted his head.

    "There," he said. He nodded toward a bench. I sat him down as gently as I could. Once we were sitting I made sure the trench coat was wrapped tight around him.

    We sat side by side and I watched the Artist intently. His eyes were trained on the two kids playing ball. We were sitting very close so that his weight could be supported by my own.

    "Yeah," he said quietly.

    There were no clouds but for some reason the sun was dull. Still, the shadows of the two children, playing fifty feet from us, stretched across the court and nearly touched our feet. Pablo sighed and the noise cut through the sound of the traffic on Cottage Grove. I felt a sharp, cold wind come into me and touch my lungs.

"It don't matter," the Artist was saying. "It don't matter, Ellison. Don't none of that shit matter now."

There was no reason for me to speak, to ask what he meant. I knew he wasn't talking to me.

"*Yeah*," he said.

Both his hands were in his lap. I could feel the struggle of his speech pass through his body and come into mine.

"All I had 'ta do is play the game the way they said it should be played. All I had to do was leave my pride right here in Chicago and they woulda gave me the whole fuckin' world." His voice was defiant but laced with irony. "But they can't say I gave 'em what they tried to take. *It cost me*, Ellison. But I neva gave any of 'em what they tried to take from me. They tried to take my soul, man."

"I know, Pablo."

"They can't *neva* say."

We both watched the two kids play. They looked like brothers. The older one was maybe ten pounds heavier. He used his weight to back down the smaller child.

The Artist laughed and said, "Beautiful."

I felt his head lift. I imagine he was staring at the sky, but I didn't turn to look at him. Instead I kept my eyes on the children

ALL FALLS DOWN

even as I felt the Artist's head come back down and rest on my shoulder.

The kids eventually stopped playing ball and I was left there with Pablo's body. A car horn blared from somewhere on Drexel Avenue. It sounded like a trumpet announcing the arrival of a king.

TWENTYFIVE

I managed to get a woman who was passing by to call the paramedics. I told the paramedics that Pablo was already dead. They asked me a lot of questions and I went to the hospital with them. They asked me more questions but most I didn't answer. I felt myself submerged in a giant fishbowl of water. I couldn't breathe and I didn't need to. The other people, the ones asking the questions and staring at me, were outside my bowl. Inside there was only me—drowning, and the word from Pablo's mouth: beautiful.

IT WAS ALMOST DARK when I got back to my apartment. There was still some media in front. I pulled the hood of my jacket up and went through the side gate.

A note had been slipped under my door. I don't know how they got in the building, but Milk Adderley was asking me to call him. The note said it was important.

Maybe I called to take my mind away from Pablo. Maybe I called because, like Kayla Forrest had told me, I was acquiring

ALL FALLS DOWN

grace, and being graceful when you are still shaking off death means calling Milk Adderley, if for nothing else than to add another interesting situation to the story you'll write and sell for millions.

A woman picked up the phone and when I told her who I was she seemed to know all about me. She asked me to meet Milk at the restaurant. My last meeting there didn't go well, I told her. But she assured me this one would be just fine. A band was performing tonight and the restaurant would be full.

I took a shower and ignored the ringing phone. I tried to eat, couldn't, and ignored the phone some more. An hour later I went out the back door feeling nothing, feeling numb, feeling as if I had actually drowned and was floating slowly to the top.

The woman I had spoken to earlier met me at the elevator outside Blu 47. She was tall, taller than me, and I thought she might be related to John Forrest. She had his gait, something I had seen before on stage and in videos, a walk that suited a hungry lion, something whose appetite could mean bad things for whoever was around it.

The room that I had seen John Forrest in that night, the one Kayla had rushed out of, was opened for me and when I went inside I saw Milk Adderely, Bells, and Tony DiSalvo.

I sat down at the table. Milk was smoking a fat cigar. Through the smoke he said, "Things done got better for you."

I looked over at Bells. He hadn't spoken and something in his ratty face told me that he had been instructed not to.

"You asked me to come. I'm here. Say what you gotta say."

No one in the small room moved or spoke.

"We'd like to make you an offer," DiSalvo said. He had been standing behind Milk and now he came forward.

"I'm listenin'."

"We'd like the video, and whatever copies have been made of it."

I smiled and shook my head. I heard what DiSalvo was saying but I was still on that bench with Pablo, watching those children play.

"I can't do that," I said.

"Of course you can," the business manager informed me. "You just take what we have for you and give us what you have."

"You could come out on top," Milk said.

I looked around the room. An amused feeling spread over me. "Where's he at?"

Everyone became surprised.

"Where's who at, Mr. Parker?"

"Your client, Mr. DiSalvo. Or did he just send you all to take care of his life?"

"Mr. Parker, we came in good—"

"I know what it is—he can't get his hands dirty. But you, Mr. DiSalvo, and you, Milk: The two of you and everybody else in this room can get dirty as hell. Don't get upset. I'm sayin' that I'm dirty too."

"Mr. Parker—"

"We'll all make sure he stays clean."

"Ellison," Milk said. "We came to talk some business."

"Then let's talk."

"We give you some compensation, you hand over them discs."

"What makes you think I have it? Did Kayla tell you she gave it to me?"

DiSalvo was frustrated. "We know Eva Vaughan sent the video to Mrs. Forrest and threatened to send a copy to the police. You brought her in yesterday and she obviously trusts you. We know she didn't give the disc to the DA because John's lawyers would have been notified by now. So that leaves you. The girl must be trusting you to hold on to the copy."

"She never gave it to me," I said. For some reason I was incapable of lying or concealing anything at that point. I was feeling outside myself and not giving a shit about what anyone in the room was saying. "I needed to get her back to the hearing and I didn't have time to convince her to tell me where she hid the copy at."

"Mutha-fucka," Bells said under his breath. His eyes were still on the floor.

"Mr. Parker, we're prepared to—"

"Forget about it. It's over. I can't give you what I don't got." I turned to Milk. "And you can call off your boys. She's with the cops."

Milk's voice was thick and heavy and absent any sort of emotion.

"What makes you think I tried to have that lil' girl kilt?"

"Someone took a shot at us."

"I don't know nothin' about that."

I was too far gone to believe him then, or to even care what he was saying.

"I'm leavin'," I told them all. "I can't give you what you want."

I got up.

"Mr. Parker—"

"—and if you want to meet with me again, tell him he has to come himself. No more of this middleman shit."

I left the room, the restaurant, and was standing outside. I felt desperate, like if I didn't keep moving something terrible would happen—my heart would cave in, or Pablo Dorsey would be sitting next to me on that bench and this time he wouldn't die quietly, he would pull me with him and spend eternity telling me all the things I should have done.

I stopped at a gas station and saw the front page of the *Tribune* through the plastic window of a newspaper box. A John Forrest headline and picture was down and to the right. A scratch across the plastic distorted his face.

I drove to Kayla Forrest's hotel. The door to her penthouse was ajar and I pushed it open. The white bodyguard was standing a few feet away from me. I looked at him and he stared back.

ALL FALLS DOWN

"Mrs. Forrest is not here."

I looked over his shoulder. "Why didn't you tell the doorman that when he called up?"

The bodyguard reached around his back. My body tensed. His hand came back with an envelope.

"She told me to give you this if you came by or mail it to you if you didn't."

He went farther inside and left me standing in front as if to give me privacy.

The letter was not written to me. It was a long, detailed account of everything that Kayla had experienced in the past month, including the mailing of the disc, the threatening note that came with it and her meeting with me. There was also the mention of the veiled threat Milk and her husband had issued to her in the back room of Blu 47 that night. The only thing left out was the night we spent together. The last page was a single note, this one written to me.

I'll contact you to explain. Until then, show this letter to no one. I can trust you.

I walked into the suite. The bodyguard had disappeared. The long windows filled the white room with light. I went to lean against one of the windows, holding the letter in my hand.

All the weight, everything I had begun to feel since Pablo had died pressed against the glass. I read the last page of Kayla's letter again. Why did she write it? Why did she give it to me?

ISAAC PERRY

I thought about dropping it on the floor, leaving it there with everything else I should have left behind.

But still, when I left the room, I took the letter with me.

TWENTYSIX

The three hours or so that passed between the time I left Kayla Forrest's suite and the moment I ended up ringing Sydney's bell are, in my memory, only a few minutes. I remember leaving the Gold Coast and going back to the hospital to get the rest of Pablo's things and finding the half-bottle of Hennessy he had hidden there. I drank most of it in my living room while I read some old short stories I had written. I played a Jazz CD but then switched it to the John Forrest album I liked the most, *Layers*. He sang so beautifully that it was hard for me to imagine him ever doing wrong. He rewrote the lyrics of sanctity and sin. I was drunk but I recognized the power of that sort of gift, the power to define reality without ever having to suffer from it.

I listened to the whole CD and then got into my car.

It must have been around eleven or twelve when I pushed Sydney's buzzer. I pressed it hard and long once, then twice, and finally she answered.

It's me.
Who?
Me.
El?
I'm drunk.
I'll buzz you up.
No.
Pablo—.
Pablo's dead, Syd.
Press against the door, Ellison.
Pablo's dead, Sydney.
Ellison, you have to press against
Syd...
Pablo's   dead.
(I closed my eyes and my head started to throb.)
Sydney, ain't I everything you want?
Wait a minute, sweetie, and I'll come down.
Syd: Ain't I everything you want?
(She didn't answer.)
Sydney?
I'm on TV!
Shit, they offered me $550,000! I'm everything you ever wanted.
I did everything
I told you I was gonna do.
I—I—I'm gonna—

ALL FALLS DOWN

The door opened. I saw Sydney's face in the dark. I felt a cold wave of shame. And then I was mad at myself and feeling sad about Pablo all at the same time.

I SLEPT IT OFF ON SYDNEY'S COUCH and dreamt about Eva Vaughan. We were at the park where Pablo had died and I was watching Eva play basketball. She was shooting lazily by herself. The ball lilted through the air, heavy as the sun, and came through the rim. Eva smiled. I sat underneath the mural, watching her as if she had brought me there to show me something. Her body moved in slow motion and every movement was left languishing in the air, like a stain that fades away slowly when you rub it. I took my eyes from her for a moment and saw Pablo on the bench by himself. I stopped smiling, stopped feeling good, and the distance between where I sat and where Pablo was dead grew until I couldn't see him anymore.

When I woke up it was nearly three in the morning. Sydney's apartment was as fly as I remembered. Everything was in place, clean and in order. The rooms smelt like cinnamon. Outside the bay windows I could see Lincoln Park.

I went into Sydney's room and sat on the edge of her bed and watched her for a while. She woke up a few minutes later and smiled at me.

"Remember when you'd be up late writing and you'd come to bed this way?" she said.

"And you'd wake up and smile at me just like that."

"Just like this." She pulled the sheets down next to her. "Come here."

I lay down with her.

"I don't think I've ever seen you drunk."

"It don't happen often."

Sydney stroked my brow. Her black tangled hair was against a white pillow. There was just a little light in the room coming from the glow of her alarm clock.

"What are you going to do, Ellison."

"I don't know."

"What's wrong?"

"I don't know how to say it."

"But you feel bad."

"I feel like shit."

She touched my cheek. "It could just be that you're tired. A lot has happened."

"I should be happy. I am happy. But I got a hole in my chest."

"Because of your friend."

"Yeah," I said. "I was with him when he died."

Sydney pulled me closer. "Come here."

We got into a position that let me lay my head on her breast. I was staring at the ceiling.

"If it ain't this, then what could it be?" I asked.

"I don't understand."

"If it ain't this—if this isn't what I'm supposed to have, then

ALL FALLS DOWN

what? When I was with Pablo, on that bench, I felt...I felt...I can't explain it, Sydney. Nothing seems complete anymore. Everything I thought I wanted. None of it seems complete."

"Don't talk like that, Ellison. Everything is going so good for you right now."

I don't know if I was still drunk. I thought I'd slept it all off. But when I raised my head a little to look at Sydney I was disoriented, lost in a way that was so purely metaphorical it shook me to my core. I was in the arms of a woman I once loved to the point that I thought every one of our passions was shared, every one of our dreams in sync. When she was gone the vacuum of her absence sucked away my idealism. And now I was looking into her face, hoping she would say or do something that would replace what I'd lost. Instead all I saw was someone I didn't know anymore, someone who couldn't offer me the promise I used to find every night in our bed and on mornings when the day itself threatened to kill me once I stepped outside my door.

"Sydney," I said quietly. "I still love you."

She just stared at me. Maybe she thought it was the alcohol.

"I'm not drunk. I love you and I know that you're happy for me. We're both different than we were, now. Both of us. And there's no going back."

"Be happy for that, Ellison."

I kissed Sydney. Her lips were dry and she pulled back. She licked her bottom lip to moisten it and then bent down to let me kiss her again. After I finished I stroked her cheek.

"Tell me what else has happened," Sydney asked.

"I'm going to New York tomorrow. I'm gonna be on the *Today* show." We were speaking very softly, intimately, like lovers who didn't want anyone to hear our secrets.

"Ellison, that's wonderful, baby."

"But, this thing with Kayla and John Forrest. It's not over."

"Maybe," Sydney said, still holding me in her arms, "but you said Kayla destroyed the disc."

"She probably did. But she left me this." I pulled the letter from my pocket and let Sydney read it.

"That's strange," she said after she'd finished.

"Part of me wants to figure it out. Part of me don't care no more."

"But the more you know about—"

"—The more I can put into a book, the more I can talk about on some talk show. I know. And there's still that other disc. I know Eva would tell me where it is if I could talk to her again."

Sydney was tracing a line around my face.

"You did more than you set out to do, El. You found that girl."

"Yeah," I said. "I found her."

"Get some sleep. Tomorrow you can figure out your next move."

I thought for a minute. "That's all anyone does. They think

ALL FALLS DOWN

about the next move. And forget the moment."

I felt sleepy again.

"You'd be proud of me, Syd. I been makin' moves."

IN THE MORNING SYDNEY AND I went to my apartment so I could pack a bag. I let the few photographers who were in front take my picture as I walked in. They shouted questions that I didn't answer but I smiled and tried to look affable.

We were driving to Midway when I looked over at Sydney and smiled. Somehow, in all of this, we had become friends. Her expectations of me had finally been met. I had achieved the secret hope that she'd always held for me, but we both knew it was too late. Now that I had it I would never give her what she had found so lacking in me before. My success was both my offering to her, and my middle finger. We loved each other, but we were too different. And although I recognized the difference between us, at that moment I didn't appreciate the cost of that difference. I didn't understand what I'd have to pay for entering her world.

I had an hour or so before my plane left so Sydney and I had coffee at a café on the lower level of the terminal. I'd been stared at more than once and approached twice so we found a spot in the rear, away from the crowd. A TV was perched above some tables and the news was on.

"Tomorrow they'll be looking at you on *Today*," Sydney laughed.

"Imagine that."

I was trying to be happy. I decided my head had to be clear to focus on the future and all the opportunities that were in front of me.

"How long will you be in New York?"

I sipped my coffee. The heat of it burned the tip of my tongue. "A few days, maybe a week. I gotta line up some meetings and get some things done while I'm there. Fifteen minutes of fame is just that."

"You're gonna have more than fifteen minutes, El. I'm sure of it."

"That's only because you love me. No one in New York loves me."

"That can't be true," Sydney said and smiled coyly at me.

"I have to get back anyway, for Pablo's funeral. I've got to make the arrangements." The word *beautiful* tried to form in my mind. I looked around the café. Some of the people talked at their tables. Others watched the television. The corridor across from us was busy with travelers walking, rushing here and there, seeking planes.

Sydney motioned me back to the TV. "They're talking about the trial." An off-camera reporter, a woman, was speaking over film of the courthouse action.

That's when I saw him.

My heart beat funny—uncertain.

I didn't know his name. But I knew his face.

My heart was going fast now. I stood up.

"What's wrong?"

I moved from our corner to the TV. The reporter's voice said:

Forrest himself will most likely not be in court today...is primarily a date set for the prosecution to deliver....Stopping just short of admitting the DA's office is interested in....Reporters asked Downey if he had spoken to...

The face in the crowd was intimately familiar. And I realized where I'd seen him before.

Sydney had come to stand next to me. "What's wrong, baby?"

"I know him."

She looked to where I was pointing. On screen was the image of several reporters surrounding ADA Downey on the courthouse steps. They all fought to get a question in whenever the prosecutor had finished answering the last one; all of them, except one reporter. He stood to the side, almost out of the picture, with his mouth closed tightly.

"You know him?" Sydney asked. I could hear the whispery chatter of the people in the café who had spotted and recognized me.

"I do." My chest felt hollow. "He tried to kill me and Eva."

TWENTYSEVEN

The blank billboard of a face stared out at me as if from some rooftop that only I could see. He was there, on the television posing as a reporter and I had seen him posing before, in the back of Father Capo's church on the West Side the day I had gone there to find Eva Vaughan.

And then I knew, instinctively because nothing else made sense, that it was him who had tried to kill us that day and it was him who had followed Sydney, Kayla and me from Blu 47. His face was just as blank, just as emotionless as it had been in that alley when I mistook him for a city worker.

I went through a door...into the alley. A white man was reading the gas meter. He wrote something down on his clipboard... and looked at me like he was afraid. I forgot about him and went into the church.

I remembered the white man's voice that had called my apartment the night I went to the party at Blu 47. He'd asked for Eva Vaughan.

"We gotta go." I took Sydney by the arm.

ALL FALLS DOWN

"What?"

"We gotta get to the courthouse."

"What are you talking about?"

I stopped and faced her.

"I saw that same man outside the church that I found Eva in. Do you understand? It was *him* that was shooting at us!"

"The reporter?"

"He ain't a reporter. He was dressed as a gas worker the day I saw him. I don't know who the fuck he is. But it had to be him that chased us that night after you and me and Kayla left Blu. He's been following me ever since."

We ran to the parking garage and I climbed in the driver's side. I didn't know exactly what I'd do when I got there. I'd have to find Downey, convince him to talk to the police and have them grab the fake reporter.

When we got to the courthouse the steps were empty. No film crews. Sydney went to park the car and I rushed into the building.

When I got inside, the hallway was filled with a mob of people crushing in both directions. I was immediately thrown into a fight, pushing against the people who pushed against me and feeling my shoulders being grabbed on and my face brushed against.

Someone screamed, "What the fuck!"

There was yelling and loud voices, a gargle of panic that seemed to spread and seep inside me. Fear and rage choked the air. A group of people began to push past me toward the doors I had just come through and I saw a band of security guards come up and throw them open. I tried to get past but the tide kept on like that—me pushing forward and the throng pushing me back.

A cop screamed, "Everyone out! Everyone out!"

A man was shoved into me and I almost fell over. Above the heads in front of me I saw cameras being held high to videotape the chaos.

I finally came to a corner and it was there where the crowd broke. Running down the hallway in groups of two or three were workers, reporters, civilians, and cops. I saw ADA Downey standing against a wall, breathing hard and shallow.

"Lock this area down! Lock—"

The cop who was yelling orders grabbed my arm as I went toward Downey and tried to take me the other way. I pushed the cop and Downey looked up.

"Wait!" he said. "Let him past!"

I walked over to Downey.

The white man's eyes were pale, almost clear and traced with only a hint of blue. His face was taut and pasty and his chest rose and fell quickly. I looked at him, knowing something that I could not know yet, possessed by the sort of understanding that runs through you when you are aware a terrible thing has happened even before you are told what it is.

The Assistant DA raised his arm. He pointed past my

shoulder, farther down the adjoining hall. I walked slowly, hesitantly while others rushed by in both directions at my sides, and I came to where she lay on the floor surrounded by paramedics and some police.

Eva's chest was covered in blood that looked wetter than any liquid I had ever seen. The glare from the hall lights reflected brightly in it and the same glare curved around her face and shined in her eyes. Her lips were parted as if she were trying to breathe but her chest was still and the two gaping holes were too much for anyone to have survived. I felt myself sway and the noise from the yelling and commotion around me was fading. I moved forward and looked into Eva's eyes again and her eyes stopped me from moving any closer. She lay there, unmoving, pretty in a white shirt that had been bludgeoned into red, and stared at me. *Close your eyes, baby.*

"Close—close her eyes."

No one heard me.

"Close her eyes!"

The people around Eva looked at me.

"Please," I said. "Close her eyes."

A cop was behind me and he took my arm. I was led away from her. I was standing next to the ADA again. A medic was standing next to him.

The first few times Downey spoke to me I couldn't respond. The noise of the hallway had been replaced in my ears by a shrill screeching sound, a steady tone that tore at my sense of place and time. I turned back around and saw Eva at the end of the hallway and I felt like caving in on myself. And then I felt rage.

"Who did this?"

Downey said, shaking his head, "A guy, he just—had a gun—he—"

"A reporter," I said.

The ADA looked at me strangely. "How'd you know that?"

"I should—" My thoughts were vague. "I should come with you."

A cop rushed up to Downey and whispered something in his ear.

"Not here," the ADA said. "Get us back to headquarters. I'm fine." He said the last part to the medic. He told the cop, "He's riding with us," and motioned toward me. We walked away. Before I lost sight of Eva I turned and looked at her again. It seemed like she was speaking to me over the space of death and other people.

I CALLED SYDNEY'S CELL PHONE from the car Downey and I rode in. I told her what had happened and asked her to meet me at police headquarters.

I stood in a room with four cops, the ADA and another lawyer. The cops were mumbling behind me. I faced a glass wall that I was told in the next room looked like a mirror. In that room were two more cops and the white man who had shot Eva. He was slender, older looking than he probably was, thin-faced and pale. He had an ordinary air to him, a nondescript presence whose only noticeable feature was his lack of any noticeable feature. He was still wearing the suit he had put on to appear as a reporter. The men sitting in front of him were asking hard questions and their voices boomed against the glass. But the murderer stared off in the distance, his eyes wide and shocked as if he had just come back from a war.

One of the cops in my room put his hand on my shoulder. He was a big burly white man, scruffy looking like the prototypical cop you see in gangster flicks. His shirtsleeves were rolled up and a notepad stuck out of his breast pocket.

"Like I said, he didn't even try to run," the cop told me. Downey and some of the other police were discussing something at the table behind us.

"We still don't know how he got the gun in. He came right up on her and squeezed off two rounds before somebody could get to him. Couple of uniforms pinned him to the floor."

"Who is he?" I asked.

"James Hoover. From North fuckin' Dakota. No priors. Been in the city for seven months. I sent some men to his apartment. Downey tells me you've seen him before."

"He shot at me and Eva, at the church."

"He got on you when you went to visit Kayla Forrest. He's told us that much. He was on Mrs. Forrest for a while, following her from her hotel. Don't know how the hell he even knew she was staying there but these crackpots figure out ways to get information, you know what I'm saying? But anyway, he must have paid somebody at the hotel a lot of money to find out who was visiting Mrs. Forrest. Once he had your name he got your address and phone number off the Internet and started following you around. That's what got him to that church."

"And to Eva," I said.

Three more cops came into our room. The burly cop that had been talking to me went over to the table. Then he called me over.

"You should see this."

On the table were digital prints of photos the cops had taken at James Hoover's apartment. Pictures of his den, his living room and his bedroom. There were photos of John Forrest on every wall, covering two-thirds of the apartment, snapshots ripped from magazines, newspapers, offline, posters, and ads.

"Jesus Christ," burly cop said.

"We're cataloging his file cabinets. Lieutenant, the guy's got at least six drawers packed full of stuff on Forrest. Magazines, tour books—I mean, every fucking thing you could imagine."

Brian Downey was staring at the mass of photos like he didn't understand what he was seeing. "He did it for Forrest."

The burly lieutenant shook his head. "The guy's a wack job. He did it for his self."

A uniformed cop burst into the room. Burly cop went over to talk to him. When he turned back around his face was stone.

"What?" Downey asked.

ALL FALLS DOWN

"They found the priest in the trunk of Hoover's car."

Everyone's head fell but I kept my eyes on the lieutenant. He looked at me with a grave air. "That's two counts of first degree."

I turned back to the glass. James Hoover was fumbling with his hands nervously. The cops were yelling questions at him. Hoover's eyes came toward me as he stared at his reflection.

TWENTYEIGHT

I had Sydney take me to the hospital where they had already pronounced Eva Vaughan dead, but they wouldn't let me see her. I sat in the waiting room with Syd for nearly an hour for no real reason. My head swam and I couldn't take the thought of getting back into a car.

"We should go, Ellison."

I didn't answer her. When I finally got up, my body rose while something in me still sat down.

"Can you take me one other place, Syd?"

"Of course."

I took out the paper I'd written Eva's mother's address on. "79th and May."

We pulled up in front of a three-flat hugged between two larger buildings. I asked Sydney to wait for me and I went to the front door and pushed the buzzer marked "Vaughan." A young woman answered and I told her who I was. She said she was Eva's cousin.

"I'd like to talk to Mrs. Vaughan."

ALL FALLS DOWN

"She in the back. We just found out an hour ago."

The cousin went into another room and I stood in front. The TV was on one of the news networks but the volume was muted. On the screen was a clip of John Forrest performing on an awards show. They segued from that into a recording of the chaos at the courthouse.

The cousin came back and said: "In here." I followed her through a series of small rooms and we ended in the kitchen.

At a table was a woman who I knew was Eva's mother because her face was Eva's face, but much older and nowhere near as pure or afraid. Mrs. Vaughan's face was in pain, but it was an experienced face and I knew that the creases and lines that were there now because she had been crying had been there before, at the news of some other loved one's death, or at some other juncture of a hard life.

"Mrs. Vaughan," I said. "I'm—"

"I know who you are."

Her voice was worn by emotion.

"I'm sorry about your daughter."

She looked up at me as if to see if I was telling the truth.

"How'd you know to come here?" she asked.

"Eva gave me the address. I talked to her the other day. She asked me to come and talk to you."

"'Bout what?"

"This case I think. She wanted you to understand why she was doing what she was doing."

Mrs. Vaughan started to cry.

"The police called here an hour 'go! Told me—my lil'—my lil' girl—was *gone*! Gone!"

The cousin rubbed Mrs. Vaughan's back for a few minutes and then the older woman looked up at me.

"That all you come here to say?" She put her head down. "I got family comin' to take me to—to identify my child's body."

"I just wanted to tell you I was sorry. I am sorry. And to tell you that Eva was doing the right thing."

Mrs. Vaughan turned hateful eyes toward me.

"I *told* her what to do. I told her how to handle all this."

"We had it handled," the cousin said from behind the mother. "She wouldn't 'a ever been in that courtroom."

I felt a pang of disorientation, as if I had swam only a few feet away from a shore and looked back to see that there was no land in sight. "I don—I don't understand."

Mrs. Vaughan shook her head. "I blame myself. *I blame myself.* I shoulda been more ad'ment with that girl."

"What do you mean when you say 'we had it handled'?"

The cousin frowned up as if she had decided not to speak to me anymore.

Mrs. Vaughan began crying again and I decided to leave.

"Again, I'm so sorry for your loss. I just wanted to come by because I told Eva I would."

I turned to walk out of the kitchen.

"I should have gotten rid of that video. Lord knows I shoulda!"

I turned back around and looked at Mrs. Vaughan. "What did you say?"

She shook her head. She was bent over, looking at the floor. "*Lawd!*"

I looked up at the cousin. "You know about the disc?"

Mrs. Vaughan broke into a fit of sobs. I could barely hear the young woman above the older one's wailing.

"We know," the cousin said defiantly.

I thought for a moment. "Then you know where the copies are. The police could use those now. With them they could still prosecute John Forrest. All of this, everything Eva went through, won't be in vain."

"'In vain?'" the young girl said. "Eva knew what she was doin'. She knew he was recording them when they was together."

"That doesn't matter does it? I know she was too embarrassed before, but now—"

"Now," Eva's mother said, "my daughter ain't gonna be all over TV makin' love to no grown man. It wasn't supposed to go that far."

I felt a trembling sensation grow in my throat. "What do you mean by that?"

Mrs. Vaughan sucked up her sobs. "She stole that video to protect herself. She needed proof of what was goin' on."

"Did you know she sent a copy to Kayla Forrest? Did you know she was threatening to send one to the police? How come she didn't come here with you when your house was burned down? Why did—"

"That's enough! I don't know you and I don't know what you tryin' to do! My daughter is dead and—and—"

"Shhh," the cousin said. "It's OK, Auntie."

The older woman looked up at me with the sort of defiance and self-assuredness that only the very old and the very young possess. I tried to match her stare but couldn't.

I had more questions but it was clear she wasn't going to give me more answers. I left the kitchen and went through the front room. When I was almost to the door I looked up and saw something that made me stop. It was an antiquated Royal typewriter. Its black skin was chipped and its metal was scarred but it sat on a shelf as if it had just been used. I heard Eva's cousin coming up behind me.

"That's just Auntie's stuff from they house," she told me. "You should leave now."

I ran my fingers across the typewriter. The note came forcefully into my mind:

NEXT VIDEO POLICE

I took out the slip of paper I'd written the house's address on and put it in the typewriter. I typed the word "next." It was

ALL FALLS DOWN

perfect to the memory of the type I'd seen on the note Kayla had shown me. I took the paper out and felt the back of it.

"This is Mrs. Vaughan's typewriter," I said.

"Yeah," the cousin answered.

I paused. "Where's the second video?"

The cousin's face tried to go blank. "I don't know—"

"No, you do know. Where's the disc you said you were gonna send to the police?"

The cousin shook her head, her eyes got teary and she refused to answer me.

"There ain't no other disc," Mrs. Vaughan said. She came to stand beside her niece. "There ain't nothin' left to prove he didn't have no business havin' sex with some young girl. I told Eva we was gonna make him pay for this. Lord knows she wasn't in the right frame of mind."

I swallowed the lump that had formed in my throat. "It was you. You sent that disc to Kayla Forrest and that note to her husband about the copy. After the fire. After Eva had run away. That's why she never admitted it to me. She didn't know it'd been sent. But once I told her, she knew it had to be you."

For a moment Mrs. Vaughan decided not to explain anything to me. But then her head nodded as if accepting an inner command she'd given herself.

"This was your *daughter*," I said.

"I know who she is!"

My eyes narrowed. "Then why the hell would you—"

"All they had to do was *pay*! Eva come to me after her and that man had been together for a while and told me everything. Said he videotaped them in his apartment. So I told her to get a hold of the recording, and she did! And all they had to do was pay. That's all! They pay us something and we give them that disc back. But he *refused*. He told her he was John Forrest and ain't nobody gonna believe what she had to say, video or no video! So I tells Eva to just wait and he'll come around but she keeps talkin' about how hurt she feels and how this whole thing is wrong. But I told her: you *grown* now. You slept with that man on your own decision. Now we got to make the best out of the situation that we can."

"But she went to the cops," I said. "She decided not to wait and went to the cops with all the letters and jewelry he gave her, telling them about their relationship."

"That prosecutor," Mrs. Vaughan continued. "Downey. He already had his heart set on puttin' John in jail one way or another. He says he had some 13 year-old lil' girl a few years ago who said John slept with her at a party. He was ready to listen to anything Eva had to say. That's the way John and Eva met—at some party she didn't have no business bein' at. She told me he started buying her things and invitin' her to his home. He seduced her."

"And you decided to blackmail him."

"After Eva gone to the police that man had somebody burn

our house down! I come home and everything *I got* is gone! What was I supposed to do? I sent a copy of that disc to his wife. Eva took the original one with her when she run away."

"She told you she had it?"

"She said she may go on and give it to the police. Or maybe not."

I thought about Saint Catherine's. If Eva hid the disc at the church then it was still there.

"That man DiSalvo called me," Mrs. Vaughan said. "We even agreed to a number. But Eva the only one knew where the copy of the disc was. I told him that."

That explained why Milk and DiSalvo were so sure I could get them the video. They'd figured that since I'd found Eva, I'd found it as well.

"The disc was just a way of keeping us out of court," Mrs. Vaughan continued. "Eva drops the case and everybody would be happy. That's all we had to do."

My head was still swimming. "That's all you had to do? That's all? What about protecting your daughter? What about not selling her to the highest fuckin' bidder? She came to you for help and all you do is teach her how to extort? She didn't want more of John Forrest's money. She wanted to stop being used. And all you did was use her some more."

Eva's mother came very close to me. I could feel the hatred in her eyes and hear it in her voice but somehow it didn't seem meant for me. "I loved her. And that's more than you can say.

Who are you to come into this house and accuse me of anything? I saw you on TV, struttin' around and giving interviews about my daughter! *Who the fuck are you?* Use somebody? What else have you done for my daughter other than use her and stand by while she gets herself killed?"

I shook my head and tried to catch my breath. "That's not what happened. I tried—"

"Get out of here," Mrs. Vaughan told me. "Get the hell *out* of here."

SYDNEY DROVE ME HOME. She didn't want to leave but I made her go. I didn't want to have to explain it but some of what I was feeling was toward her. She didn't know, maybe she couldn't understand it, but she was like the rest of them in my mind. She was one of them. So I kissed her on the cheek in her car and told her I would be all right. Before I got out she touched my arm.

"I know it doesn't feel like it now, Ellison, but things will be better in the morning. It's not like before, when things would go wrong and you wouldn't have no way of fixing them. You have a way now. You're in control."

I looked into Sydney's cool eyes.

"Ain't none of us in control, Sydney. I know you want to pretend it's that way, but you know it ain't." I shook my head. "'Everywhere you go, there you are.'"

I got out of the car and shut the door. There were no re-

ALL FALLS DOWN

porters. Through the glass I saw Sydney's face mixed with the reflection of the buildings behind me. She raised her hand to say goodbye. We both knew that it would be a long time before we saw each other again.

I lay down in my bed. It was mid-afternoon but the light outside was gray. I smelt something strange and started to think about Eva. I realized that my sheets still smelled of her and I bent my nose down into them and inhaled. I turned to lie on my stomach so my face was deep in the pillow. I wanted to go to sleep but there were questions still alive in my head and all of them burst open at the same time.

Brian Downey called.

"I thought you'd want to know, James Hoover gave a full statement." He let out a breath. "My office will be seeking the death penalty."

"Father Capozziello was well loved," I told Downey.

"It's not just for him, Mr. Parker. I would have sought this sentence even if Eva were the only victim."

"How did Hoover kill Capo? In the church I heard someone call his name and he went out, saying he needed to talk to a parishioner."

"His statement says he saw you go in the rear of the church and he went around to a window and saw you, the priest and Eva talking together in a room. He goes back into the alley but one of the kids from the rec center is back there smoking a cigarette. If you remember he was dressed as a gas technician. So he gets this kid to go in and ask Father Capo to come out on the pretense that he needed to speak with him about the church's gas readings. Capo comes out, tells the kid to get back in the rec center, and he and Hoover talk. His story gets a little fuzzy right there. Our psychologist thinks this guy's rage distorts his memory, especially if the memory involves violence. But at any rate, he kills the Father—that is, he stabbed him several times with a blade we found in his car—and puts him in the trunk. He goes back to the window to see if you and Eva are still inside. Now we're back into the rage. He tries to kill both of you because he knows you're 'plotting' against John Forrest. Incidentally, everything I've told you constitutes the first four pages of his statement. The next *twelve* are about Forrest. Hoover's obsessed with him."

"Why didn't he just come into the church instead of shooting through the window?"

"He says, and I quote this, 'I ain't no sinner to be shootin' up a church.' He told the cops it was alright to kill Capozziello because the Father was working for evil."

Downey continued. "He's been on this for months. We found evidence he paid a cop to get him the information on Eva. But he didn't confess to the arson."

I thought about the disc that Mrs. Vaughan said Eva still had. "Did the police get Eva's things from Saint Catherine's? Did they find any other evidence?"

"No," Downey answered, his voice slightly suspicious.

"They bagged all her belongings but we didn't find anything out of the ordinary. Were you expecting us to?"

"Not at all." I was ready to get off the phone. "Looks like you'll have to find another way to get to John Forrest, counselor."

"I plan to," he said, and I guessed that his determination had very little to do with justice for Eva Vaughan. Like everyone involved in the scandal ADA Downey had his own ambitions.

An appointment was made for me to come in and speak on record about what happened at the church. I hung up and thought about the disc, wondering where Eva had hidden it, wondering if it would ever be found.

I got out of bed a while later and found Kayla's cell number.

"I need to talk to you."

"Now is not a good time," she said.

"I don't care. I need to talk to you."

She was quiet.

"Meet me at the hotel. I'm here."

I got my keys and went downstairs.

I parked in the same garage I'd parked in the first time I'd visited her. Michigan Avenue was hung over. Gray clouds moved above me like floating migraines. I went up the sixty-four flights and Kayla answered the door herself.

A part of me wanted to blame Kayla for everything that had

happened. It was irrational, but I was still in the throes of denial. I wanted someone else to explain to me how Pablo could have died anonymously yet content, and how I had failed to live that way. I wanted someone to explain Eva's blood and my part in it. I'd named Kayla my mentor, so it fell on her to make sense of everything, to explain her world to a careless tourist.

Kayla's penthouse suite had been completely redone: the white furniture had been replaced by multicolored fusions that were dark, sultry and moody. There was an Asian feel to the décor. Kayla was wearing a tight, crimson dress that made her curves even longer than they were and seemed to sweep them away from her body, into the room itself.

She closed the door behind me and we both walked to the windows as if we were going to our marks on a stage.

"What are you doing here?"

"I came to see you."

"I know that much." She stared at me emotionlessly.

I nodded toward the room. "You changed up."

"They did it all in one day," Kayla said. She gave the room a vague glance. "It was time."

I made my voice warm. "Did you destroy the disc?"

"Yes. The same night I told you I would."

She looked out the window, disinterested. It had started to rain.

"This ain't no good, Ellison."

"Say it."

ALL FALLS DOWN

"It's over. Everything is over."

I nodded my head. "You're right. She's dead. Now all your problems are solved."

Kayla tried to slap me but I caught her hand. She stood in front of me breathing hard and looking at me with angry eyes.

"Relax," I told her. "Remember how much trouble that got us into the first time."

Her eyes slipped from anger into pain and then she turned them away from me.

"I'm going to get a drink," she said. "Do you want a drink?"

I grinned, shook my head, but told her, "Yes."

She made us both martinis and we sipped them by the window as it kept on raining.

"I saw you on the news," Kayla said. "I guess I didn't give you enough credit." She grinned maliciously, mocking me. "I thought you were innocent."

"No," I said, "I was never innocent."

Kayla sighed and her body seemed to be less tense. "I don't know what to say to you."

"Say what you feel."

"I feel tired. I feel sad because—because of everything that's happened."

A subtle hope stirred inside me, the kind of hope created by the denial of loss. "It's not too late, Kayla. You could still try to make the best of this."

"I am making the best of this," she told me. She stared at me with warm compassion. "Don't you remember what I told you that night in the park? I'm doing what I have to do."

I looked away.

"Ellison," she said, reaching toward me. "Tell me what you're doin' here."

"I'm not sure," I said. "I came before and you had left that letter."

"I want you to keep it. It's insurance for both of us."

"This is a game to you."

She cracked a thin smile. "If I thought this was a game, I wouldn't play so hard. I know exactly what this is, and so do you."

"No," I replied. "You were right, I don't have what you have, or what your husband and his friends got."

"I saw you on TV. I've watched how you worked this whole thing to your advantage. Maybe I was right before, but now—" She stopped and put her hand against my cheek. "Now you've shown me who you really are."

We kissed, or more accurately, we tried to devour each other. I felt the same insane urgency that she had inspired in me before, mixed with a self-contempt that was growing at a fast pace. When we pulled away from each other Kayla was panting short, quick breaths and I was glaring at her passionately, or furiously. I'd never felt as crazy as I did at that moment. In one woman was everything I desired and everything

ALL FALLS DOWN

I'd learned to resent. I could have made love to her, or thrown her out the window.

"I'm not like you," I said out loud. But it wasn't a statement; it was an affirmation.

"Come to the bedroom," Kayla said. "One last time."

I was full of the need for her, remembering the graze of her nipples against my lips even as her breasts pressed against me, my free hand slipping down to rub her hip, remembering what was underneath, everything about her body unfurling in my mind, the need to be inside her again out of control. She brought her mouth up to my neck and was kissing me there. The hand she wasn't holding her drink in had made its way between my legs.

"Baby," she said, "just one more time."

I took a step back from her and stood there breathing hard, wild inside, too many emotions rushing through. My head started to move side to side as if I was saying "no." Kayla stared at me like I was a stranger who had suddenly appeared in her house. Her beautiful, heavy face was confused and nervous. I raised the martini glass in front of me, holding it between us.

"Take this," I said.

Kayla took my glass. I turned and walked toward the front door.

"Ellison!" Kayla screamed, "I'm sorry about that girl. I'm sorry about all of it! But I earned what I got. I earned my life, Ellison!"

I turned around and looked at John Forrest's wife. She stood with her legs wide, in a fighter's stance.

"Some of that's true," I said.

I went out and closed the door. Before I could take my hand away from the knob I heard the sound of a martini glass break apart against the other side.

TWENTYNINE

I drove around downtown, looking at Chicago. I had fallen in love with it a long time ago. I was ten years old, riding in the back seat of my cousin's car, and it was Gotham City: the canyons of the Loop seeming straight out of a comic book. As I drove around the curve of the river and turned onto LaSalle I realized I had come to know the city intimately. I understood the language the skyscrapers spoke where before I had just heard their sounds. I related to the city's paradox, I knew how it had become world famous yet still unknown.

I went to Randolph where the West Loop restaurants were getting ready for the dinner crowd. I waited in the traffic on Canal and watched the after-workers walk in throngs to Union Station. Then I drove north again and sat for a while near the park on Pearson Street. The lights of the Mile were beautiful as usual, a sort of nightly celebration of capitalism that was profound and disturbing.

When I couldn't completely quiet the things in my head I went home.

○ ○ ○

THAT NIGHT PABLO DORSEY SAT ON A BENCH in the snow in Dayton, near the house I grew up in. I wasn't in the dream but still he looked up at me and tried to say something. But the wind was blowing too hard, and snow filled his mouth before he could speak.

I woke up around 2 am and heard the phone ringing. The Caller ID was blank so I didn't answer. I scrolled through all the numbers and saw that Marie had called seven times that day.

I poured a glass of orange juice and went to sit behind my computer. I fell asleep in the chair and the phone woke me again in the morning. It was Tony DiSalvo.

"I'm calling on behalf of Mrs. Forrest. She says she gave you something."

I'd wondered how long it would take Kayla to tell them about the letter.

"It's early."

"We'd like that item back, Mr. Parker."

"You should," I said. "It could have every one of you in jail."

DiSalvo was silent.

"I'll tell you what. I'll give you the letter back. But only if your client comes for it himself. No one else. Not even you. Just him."

"That's not acceptable."

I hung up.

ALL FALLS DOWN

DiSalvo called back ten minutes later.

"My client has agreed to your request, Mr. Parker. But he will not come alone. This is not an interview."

"Don't tell me what the fuck this is."

"Nonetheless," DiSalvo continued, as if I had said nothing, "we'd like to wrap this up today. At the restaurant."

"Today."

"This afternoon, at five."

He was playing me. John Forrest would never show up to retrieve a letter that could implicate him in the very case that he had just beaten. But I agreed to the meeting anyway. I needed an ending.

Later that day I found the letter and read it again. Kayla said she'd given it to me as insurance, probably for her to use in case her husband didn't agree to whatever terms she had demanded when she went back to him. But she had to have known that I would use it, that I might have even published it. I remembered her mocking my lack of what she called "grace." My lack of all the things she said that were necessary to live in her world. According to her I possessed those things now.

I got dressed and drove to Blu 47. It was late afternoon and the sun was bright but it was definitely autumn. Halfway to the restaurant I thought about the ride I had taken a few days before with Eva. I remembered us on the steps of the courthouse and how she had looked at me.

The restaurant didn't officially open until that evening but when I got off the elevator on the second floor a woman was waiting for me. It was the same young girl I had met the night I had come to the party for John Forrest, the singer from the West Side with the dirty mouth and the pure face.

I smiled at her. "Carmen, right?"

She smiled back. She seemed more subdued than when we first met. "Thas' right." I watched her turn around. "This way."

We passed the art gallery and went into the restaurant. I expected to see DiSalvo sitting alone at a table, full of reasons why his client was not with him. But once we were inside I saw that the restaurant was empty and all the tables had been stripped and chairs were turned upside down on top of them. The entire space, in the daytime, had the weird, manic stillness of a wild animal at rest.

A man sat at the bar.

I went over and sat down on the stool next to him. He was preoccupied with a newspaper.

Another man came suddenly around the corner. He asked me if I wanted something to drink. The man next to me was drinking water so I asked for the same thing.

When I had my water I drank some of it and put the glass back on the bar top.

"Did you bring it?" Milk asked me.

"Of course."

He didn't look up.

"Good," he said. "You doin' the right thing."

ALL FALLS DOWN

That's when I started to laugh. Slowly at first. It was not very loud but it was a real laugh. And absolutely nothing was funny.

"This ain't no good." I shook my head. "We've done this before, Milk. I've been here before, and you've been here before. Now he should be here."

Milk put down his paper and finally looked at me. "You knew that was bullshit. He ain't gonna come anywhere near this again. It's over, man. It's all over."

"Someone else told me the same thing. 'It's over.'"

"They was right."

I looked at Milk for a moment and then drank some more water. I shook my head again. "No. That can't be right. 'It's over?' That doesn't feel right, Milk. It can't be over. I need you to tell me what happens next."

Milk's eyebrows raised and he spoke matter-of-factly. "You go and tell your story, minus that letter. You get your paper. You ain't gonna mention the disc because Kayla gave it to us. We talked to Mrs. Vaughan. She ain't got the copy and she said you don't have it either. So that's it. Ain't no more proof. But you still got enough shit to write a book about. They say you found that girl in a church, that the same crazy muthafucka that killed her shot at you and killed Father Capo. That sounds like a story to tell."

He picked his glass up.

"You're right," I said. My voice sounded strange. "Everything worked out for everybody."

Milk looked at me suspiciously.

"Let me see the letter."

"I can't do that, Milk."

The big man's eyes narrowed. "Ellison, I like you, man. But now you got to give up that letter. It's over."

"It ain't over. See—that's the *big lie*. It ain't over now and it won't be over if I give you this letter. And I can't give you this letter, Milk. You gotta understand that. And even if you don't understand it, you gotta accept it. 'Cause if I give you this letter, if we just walk out of here and pretend that it's really over, then no one will have ever done anything for her. We'll never hear what she was tryin' to say. It'll be like everything she did, all the reasons she hurt herself to get our attention never happened. And people like you and people like me can go on and we can even make money off this and say it's over. But that won't end it, Milk. She was trying to tell me something and I didn't listen. And *he* didn't listen. And none of us did anything about it. We made it worse for her, man. We pretended like that girl was old enough to know what the hell she was doing, and we did that because it's easier that way. That way everybody comes out on top. We keep pretending and pretty soon what's really goin' on don't matter. Not if what's really goin' on ain't makin' nobody rich. Na, reality don't matter. All we need to do is pretend. We pretended then, and I'd be pretending now if I gave you this letter."

ALL FALLS DOWN

Out of the corner of my eye I saw men entering the restaurant. Standing at the far end of the bar was the rat-faced Bells and four other men seethed in separate parts of the room.

"You can't walk out of here with that letter, El. It ain't gonna happen." Milk looked at me as if I were already dead.

I got up slowly from the bar and took a few steps. The five men took steps toward the bar and then were still.

"You think that girl was innocent?" Milk said. "She didn't deserve to die, but she wasn't never innocent. She knew exactly what she was doin'."

I felt weary deep in my bones, a tired feeling that made me careless. I didn't care if they killed me, just as long as I didn't *give* them the letter.

"You're right. She wasn't innocent, Milk. But that's because we told her she shouldn't be."

I glared at him with more hatred than he deserved.

"You want the letter? Then you tell these cats they're gonna have to go to work. Tell 'em I ain't giving it up on my own. Tell 'em they're gonna have to really fuck me up before they get it."

He didn't answer.

"Tell 'em!"

All five men moved toward us but Milk raised his hand and they stopped where they were. The big man's eyes were lowered in thought. He looked up at me. I was still breathing hard and feeling crazy.

When Milk spoke I heard a trace of the same weariness that

I felt. When I think back to it I wonder if the ripple effect of John Forrest's life had finally begun to wear on his friend.

"That letter ever turns up, you're a dead man, Ellison. There won't be no meetings, no conversations. They'll find you in Indiana, man. Missin' parts."

I looked at Milk without any emotion. Then I looked around at the men who wanted to kill me. I took a few steps but stopped when I was standing next to Milk's barstool.

"We're worse than the rest of 'em, man. DiSalvo. The press. We're worse than them because she was a part of us. We were supposed to protect her."

The big man didn't look at me. He raised his newspaper back up to his face and said, "Get out of here, Ellison."

WHEN I GOT OUTSIDE I saw Carmen Shelton on the sidewalk. She was leaning against the doorway and watching cars pass on the boulevard. When she saw me she smiled and said, "You leavin' already?"

I nodded and started to walk away. Then I looked Carmen in her eyes. "You should leave too."

A look came across her face that made her features even more attractive than they already were.

"There's nothin' but dangerous people here," I said.

I turned to go. Something told me to look back but I didn't. That look on her face was all I wanted to take with me.

ALL FALLS DOWN

o   o   o

I DROVE BACK HOME and sat at my desk looking at the letter. I decided to mail it to some other reporter one day, but I'd wait until I knew I was sending it for the right reason. For her, not for me.

I tried to write and discovered I couldn't do it. I started seven times but it wouldn't work.

I walked to the park on 63rd Street. It was cool and the sun was red while it went down. There was a group of young cats playing half-court under one of the newer rims. I sat on a bench and thought about what I had been trying to write and how Pablo, before he died, had said that people depended on him. The wind brushed against me, carrying a Lake Michigan breeze. It was gone; the only thing I really cared about was gone. And I couldn't pretend that I didn't know why.

A NOTE ABOUT THE AUTHOR

ISAAC PERRY has written for publications such as XXL, VIBE, KING, and SLAM since 1998. A native of Columbus, Ohio, Perry has traveled extensively throughout America and abroad, adding his distinctive voice to the global phenomenon of hip-hop and basketball culture.
He lives in Chicago.

WWW.ISAACPERRY.COM

A NOTE ON THE TYPE

This book was set in a typeface called Eldorado, designed by W.A. Dwiggins (1880-1956) in 1951. A graphic artist of the highest caliber, Dwiggins approached his craft with extreme seriousness and was meticulous to a fault. In Eldorado he sought to create, "...a face that should be sturdy, and yet not too mechanical." Beginning in 1942 the designer experimented with various cuts, endeavoring to create a type that stood apart from the industry norm. Influenced by a design used by 18th Century printer Antonio de Sancha in Madrid, Dwiggins produced a face that showed the subtle hint of the Spanish type, especially in the smooth cut of its arches, curves, and junctions. Notably, in the lowercase, there is a flourish of color in the serifs that is coolly balanced by the weight of some of the type's curves and finials. The roman capitals are winged with serifs that express Eldorado's innovative and elegant style.

THE INTERIOR OF THIS BOOK WAS COMPOSED & DESIGNED BY
ARTHUR TURNBULL DESIGN
CHICAGO, ILLINOIS